TIME FOR INFINITY
BOOK FOUR

ONCE
UPON
A
TIMELOOP

Brona Mills

is not suitable for anyone under the age of 1

ACKNOWLEDGEMENTS

Book four in the series, well five if we count the companion romance novel – which I of course do!
I hope you enjoy reading about Caitlyn and Liam. From the beginning, Caitlyn held a special place in my heart, like all the female characters I write, and I was so glad you guys kept asking for her story too!

Thank you to my friends and family for the encouragement along the way. And thank you to you, the people who love this world as much as I do. Without readers, we wouldn't have books.

bronamills.com

Subscribe to my newsletter for exclusive free giveaways, news on what's coming next, book covers and character development and sneak peeks at chapters before they are released!

Follow me on social media
instagram.com/bronamillsauthor/
tiktok.com/@bronamills
facebook.com/bronamillsauthor

Or join up to my readers group

PART ONE:
THE BEGINNING.
OR THE END.
DEPENDS ON WHICH WAY YOU LOOK AT IT.

PROLOGUE

CAITLYN RV 2:0
FEBRUARY 29TH 2004

CAITLYN IS 24

I thought I'd live longer. Twenty-two is hardly anything.

I'm injured, alone, in a cave, and there's not another tour group due back for another week. They don't even come down this deep.

My body might never be found.

The energy building inside here is quirky. It resonates with something deep inside me. But it's too late. It's knowledge of death now.

I thought I'd be emotional at the end of my life. Especially when I know the mistakes I made. The signs from the universe, or whatever, told me not to go here. I should have had more faith in my faith.

I let my body relax and rest my head on the ground. The hard rock underneath my skull makes the pulsing headache worse. I touch the tender side of my head. It's wet with blood, and it's not drying as it should.

Head injuries bleed a lot. My brother dated an ER nurse once. The bloody stories made the best pub talk.

When I let my eyes close, instead of the darkness I expect to help ease the pain behind my eyes, a subtle brightness shines through my lids.

When I open my eyes, a green light bounces off the cave walls. A light behind me? The brown cave walls seem closer than I realised now that I can see better. It's a tight spot. I roll to my back and it feels like I let myself drop out of a window.

It's not the rescue flashlights I thought it was. It's crackling blue lightning. It's green swirls of light. Like the northern lights, suspended in the middle of a cave. It's beautiful this close up. The shades of green and purple seem impossible, not only because there is a lack of reflection down here for lights to be appearing naturally—I learned that from hiking into a concave volcano once—but it bounces near the roof of the cave, like the lights are trying to escape and find their place in the sky. Like me. We both need to get out of here.

But we're in too deep. Literally. I couldn't even find my way out of this crevice, let alone reverse the two-hour trek I made to get down here.

I grab my backpack and hug it close to my chest.

Bottled water, energy bars, and a cell phone charger are all that's left of me. The cell phone was the first casualty in this stupid escapade. Dropped for an entire minute before I heard it contact water below. I'm not a physics major like Liam, who could probably work out the distance, based on the weight of the phone and the time to crash to the surface below.

Liam is like religion to me. Not that I'm obsessed and chant at his feet. But he's consumed so much of my life so far, though I like to pick the advice and guidance he's given me. I believed in him. But I only took the things I *liked* verbatim. The things I didn't care for, I ignored. Or pretended that he might be wrong. Or that I could prove otherwise.

My death was one of the things I ignored.

In the end, *I'm* not dying. There are other Caitlyns out there who never made these stupid decisions. There are other versions of reality where I'm tucked up in bed, or where I got back on the tour bus, or heck, maybe I've found him and the answers already.

The problem is when we realise there are lots of universes and versions out there, which one do you cling to? Which one is the right one?

I thought *this* would be the version of my life that would all work out. I guess the universe will just have to make the next one count.

CHAPTER

ONE

Nine years ago.
Caitlyn RV1:0

December 1995
Caitlyn is 16

I hate it when the guests call me a kid. I've just turned sixteen, nearly a legal adult. If I wanted to, I could hop the border to Scotland and get married.

'Now this is for you, kid,' the father of the American family says. 'You did a good job.' The last guest of winter hands me a five-pound note, and my mum smiles as she waves the family off in the taxi. We both sigh in relief. Well, mine is a relief. Mum's probably worried. Winter is tough for local businesses. The harsh weather next to the sea puts a lot of tourists off. Unless you cater to the festive crowd who party through Christmas and New Year. But Mum and Dad always close at the end of December. It's the only time off they take all year. If they decided to work fifty-two weeks straight, it might just kill them.

'Now the real work begins.' Mum nudges my side, and we walk back into the house. It's only eight-thirty, but Mum hands me a list of chores and puts her bag strap over her head.

9

'Your dad is driving me into town to get the shopping in. We'll be gone most of the day since we need to find some things for Christmas, too.'

I look down at the list of jobs for me to do and gawk. 'I'm never getting all this done. I have school, you know.' She knows. I'm standing in my school uniform, but I love to state the obvious.

'You can get it done afterwards,' she says. 'I have the committee meeting later, so I won't be home for dinner either. Help your dad cook, or you'll both starve.' She shudders.

Dad joins us at the front door. 'I can make a pot noodle all by myself.' He places his arm around Mum's shoulder and she moves towards the door, impatient as always. 'Well, you *have* screwed that up.' She rolls her eyes and opens the front door.

'Lock up when you leave,' Dad says.

I put the list on the phone console and return to the kitchen to finish my tea. I've been working in the B&B since I could carry a breakfast plate, so I've over ten years of experience. But things have gotten worse lately. Since Michael left for college. I never realised how much work he did for Mum and Dad.

After my now ten-hour days of school and chores, I've no energy left to study, let alone see my friends. I guess that's why I don't have many left. Most of the families here in Blackpool are in the tourist industry. Only they don't seem to work as much as I do. Or if they do, they at least get paid. Five pounds of pocket money a week doesn't give me much beyond one cinema trip and sweets from the shops. That used to be fun with Michael, but on my own, it's kind of crappy.

Detours after school along the harbour have become my only way to survive the nights of bickering at home. It gets dark pretty early in the winter, but I'd rather take a walk along

10

the cold and dark seafront to clear my head and give me a sense of freedom. The sound of the waves crashing against each other and battering off the pier reminds me that there's an entire world out there, and once I'm old enough, I can go exploring.

The sea is vast, and the world beyond it even greater. I've met tourists from all parts of the world, but they all have the same thing in common. They're exploring. I want to see the places they come from. See what it's like in the thick of reality in Spain, Italy, and France. To see how bad that jet lag to Australia is. To see the city buildings of America and judge for myself if it really is the greatest country of all.

Natalie at the pier is one of my few friendly interactions for the day. She bought the booth from Grandad or from Dad after Granddad died a month ago. It was quick. The sale of the booth and his death. Before the funeral, his fortune teller's booth on the pier already had a new occupant. The bleakness of my life and his death is everywhere I look.

With Christmas approaching, the city is cold and windy and miserable. Rain comes off the shore and splashes ice-cold water on my face, as well as soaking me from above. The bitterness is something you don't get used to. Despite a winter coat, snood, and gloves, there is always cold rain splashing against your face.

The door is at the side of the wood cabin, providing it with some shelter, and I enter and go through the curtain where Natalie sits with her customers for readings.

She pulls back the curtain and starts fussing over me.

'Jesus, girl, you're soaked. Don't you have a brolly?' She pulls my gloves and scarf off me and shakes them, trying to get

11

some of the rain off. Ushering me through the curtain, she lets me sit in her seat, next to the halogen heater, and I rub my hands in front of the artificial orange light.

Natalie lays my things over the other chair as she talks. 'I know you want to keep me company, but this is out of your way home from school. You don't need to get the flu for me,' she says.

I examine my red hands, which are prickling with the heat infusing into them. I don't know why Natalie stays open through winter. Most of the traders here only operate in high tourist months, finding other work during the quiet season. Maintenance jobs and road gritters are the big voids that need to be filled in the winter. As well as building and renovating work for the quieter B&Bs.

It's been years since our guest rooms were redecorated. Compared to others, it's looking drab. It's one of the many arguments I overhear Mum and Dad having. We can't afford it. Things are getting worse every year, and eventually, the house will probably just fall down. They might still argue about it even then. Who was right and who was wrong? They both still need to get the last word in.

It's exhausting just listening to them, let alone being a part of it.

'What do you do here all day with no customers?'

'I meditate,' Natalie says. 'Besides, you never know who might come knocking on the door.'

At twenty-five, Natalie is the most functional adult I know. She runs her own business, never seems harassed, and goes out with her friends on the weekend. Natalie's mother runs the fortune teller booth right next door. There are seven of them in total along the main front, scattered between souvenir shops and the occasional rock-making stand. Despite appearing to be in a competitive business with each other, all the traders on the pier help each other out. We're all dependent on the tourist industry, and if one family has a bad experience, it might just affect us all in the years to come.

Luckily, Blackpool has been one of those few places people return to year after year, and when they grow up, they bring their kids along for the same experience. Some rollercoaster rides in a small theme park, right next to the seaside, streets full of B&Bs for them to stay in, and restaurants and cafés. Sweet stalls and candy floss makers. Fresh hot doughnuts and burger stalls to snack on all day long. Souvenir shops that sell all kinds of cheap gifts to bring back home to your school friends. And the entertainment. Pubs and clubs and football matches and, of course, fortune tellers.

'Seriously, though. Today I was gathering paperwork for a course I want to apply for. There is always something for me to do. I'd rather be sitting here listening to the sea than at home listening to my mum chattering in the background.'

'Tell me about it.' I make a fist with my hands and blow into them.

'Is that why you're here?' She perches on the edge of the seat opposite me. 'You need some time for yourself?'

I shrug. I don't want Natalie to know how sucky my life has been lately. Natalie grew up in Blackpool like us all, but being ten years older than me, she was always cool.

She would bring flasks of tea and sandwiches for her mum at lunchtime and always had a spare cup for Grandad. If I was down at the pier with him for the day when I was a kid, Natalie would bring me to the pleasure beach and get us on a ride for free.

'Well, why don't you stay here while you do your homework? I have a box of things for you to look through that your grandad left here. I'll dig it out.'

Natalie rises. Behind me is a small counter where she keeps her personal items and hides things she doesn't need customers to see. No need to ruin the magic with tax documents and receipts for the year. No need for them to realise the supernatural is also a business.

I twist in my seat and wait for Natalie to pull out a couple of boxes and sift through some things, pushing bags back into their place and rejecting the first box she looked through. She pulls out a plastic container, mostly filled with paper documents, and I spot Grandad's keyrings and penknife he used to peel apples with.

'This was the most important looking thing.' She refers to a beat-up old brown envelope and hands it to me. Inside is a cassette tape, the plastic cover held together with a worn elastic band. An extra-long, thick one that the postmen use and my mum asks to keep sometimes. Those little thin ones you get in the shops break so easily. This elastic band looks like it's been used for years, and it is still holding up.

The white label on the tape reads:

TO CAITLYN. FROM LIAM.

'Who's Liam?' I ask.

Natalie purses her lips. 'I thought you would know. Sorry it took so long to get these to you. I was waiting a few weeks before I asked your mum what she wanted to do with his things here, but she said just clear everything out and bin it. But when I started, I found some receipts and business files she's going to need, and then I found that envelope. Some of the other things I kept here.' She nods over her shoulder to the old signs and pictures still hanging on the wall that used to belong to my granddad.

'You can take them. Anything you want to keep for your room, or you think your brother might want.'

I shake my head. 'No, they belong here.' I place the brown envelope and cassette on the floor next to my wet feet. 'And I know you'll look after them.'

Natalie smiles. 'It was mostly junk here. Your mum didn't mean anything by not saving it. I'm sure she didn't realise you had some of your music here.'

'It's not mine,' I tell her.

'Well, it's your name on it, so take it.'

I nod and pull out my homework. At least here, I won't have to clean five rooms before dinner.

'Want some tea?' Natalie pours me some tea from a flask she has behind the counter. I turn the cassette tape over and over in my hand, wondering why Grandad has a tape labelled up for me.

Before it gets completely dark, Natalie locks up the hut and we head back to my house together. Her uncle, George, owns the B&B next door to ours, and sometimes she goes there for dinner with her mum. The rain has stopped, and I pull my bag, heavy now with the new addition of the box Natalie gave me, up over my shoulder.

The sky is dull, and the sun is almost set, although you can't see it disappear behind the horizon of the water like a clear summer day. The streetlights flick on, and it will be pitch-dark soon.

Natalie and I go around the back street of the houses, down the narrow close of the walls at the back of the gardens, and let ourselves in through her uncle George's gate. The gardens here are small, allowing for the front of the house to have an impressive garden and view for the guests. Through the

15

kitchen window, we see George already cooking, and we rush in the back door to get out of the wind and cold.

Right as we cross the threshold, we realise, too late, that someone is with him. Snuggled under his arm and kissing his neck is my mum.

It's only when I hear the gate close behind me and Natalie calling out my name that I realise I'm running away, like it happened all on its own, and I've only just realised what my body is doing. I keep running because it's hard to breathe. And I need to concentrate on breathing. I'm on the pier front and heading to Granddad and then I realise that he's not there anymore. But his cabin gives me an escape and a place to hide. No one realises I know where he hid a spare key, and no one will think to look for me there.

It's not like I can go home. If I look at Dad, I'll start crying. And if I look at Mum, I'll start screaming. Both things require me to deal with what's happening, and right now I want to disappear.

At the end of the road, I cross over to the beachside and rush around the corner, so I won't be seen if anyone is following me. The closed stores comfort me with the familiar creak of the shutters getting battered by the wind.

At Grandad's stall—Natalie's now—I move a broken plank from the bottom of the structure and pull out the fake rock jammed inside. The key is cold, just like my hands and Mum's heart. I struggle to jam the thing into the door lock. When it finally gives way, I turn the knob and slam the door shut behind me. It's still warm in here from when we left. I lock the door behind me, so it looks like it's not been disturbed since Natalie locked up, and I slide down the doorframe.

I want to block the world out. I pull my Walkman out of my bag, and the cassette that Natalie gave me crashes to the floor. I flip it over in my hand, but apart from the *to* and *from*

16

inscription, there is only a/b scribbled on each side. I pull the door to the Walkman open, toss out the music tape I've been listening to on repeat for weeks, and slide the new cassette inside. The door cranks closed. I slide across the room and plug in the heater. Turning up the volume wheel, I climb into the seat that my grandad spent most of his life working in, selling people their future fortunes and well wishes, and listen.

Caitlyn. The voice stops a beat like the speaker is unsure of what to say. Listening to someone speak my name is a little concerning. And why did Grandad have this tape? Did he know the man attached to the voice?

It sounds strange to speak your name. We've never met. But in one life, we were supposed to. Or so I've been told.

I pause the tape and sit up straight in the chair. I look around Grandad's cabin like I'm going to find an answer to where this tape came from or the strange American man who knows my name, but I have no idea what I'm looking for.

When I shift in the seat and rearrange the blanket, I must lean on the button because the tape starts up again.

I'm assured that at one point we will meet. And we will become good friends. In the meantime, I can only tell you what I know. Or what this one version of me knows. Because there are a whole load of versions and lives and realities of me and you and everyone out there. The one I'm in right now has been kind of crappy. And you're dead before you should be. And some of our friends are in trouble.

So, you have a job to do. And I'm not even sure what it is.

Bear with me, while I start at my beginning.

Any normal person would have turned off the tapes and tossed them back into the cupboard. Some guy says I'm going to die. And it's not the worst thing that's happened

17

today. At least he sounds kind of sorry about it. I close my eyes
and listen until I fall aslee

CHAPTER
TWO

CAITLYN 2:0
ECUADOR, 2004
CAITLYN IS 24

There's a weird obsession that comes with learning
about how you're going to die. Might die. The thing I want to
know is why I felt the need to put myself in this position, just to
prove that Liam was right all along. Because *right* in this
instance means I'm dead.

CHAPTER THREE

It's easy to ignore Mum when I have my headphones on. It also makes cleaning rooms much easier when I have something to occupy my mind with.

When I woke up in Natalie's cabin last night near 10:00 p.m. and got the courage to go back home, Mum and Dad were watching TV. She hadn't told him anything.

Dad had thought I was at the cinema with a friend, a lie that only my mum could have told.

This morning, before I left for school, Mum's only question was if I intended to tell Dad. She never said she was sorry, or that she would stop seeing George. Her only concern was if I was going to keep her secret. Because if the family falls apart, we would have nowhere to live. That's what she said. *That we can't keep the house and business going with the three of us. So, there's no way neither she nor Dad can afford to divorce and live in separate houses.*

Great.

If I tell Dad, I'm the bad guy. If I don't tell Dad, I'm also the bad guy.

19

Fuck this life, and fuck her.

Natalie says karma will catch up and the truth always comes out in the end. But that's some silly wishy-washy line she and my grandad both used on the tourists.

My headphones have been firmly in place every time I step outside my room.

I've listened to the cassette tape over and over. It's a c90 tape, so that's an hour and a half worth of pondering the possibility of my death. Ironically, it's more entertaining that changing bedsheets.

After the first few hours, I had a headache by the end of listening. Over and over, the same voice. The same words of warning. The same crazy talk about alternative realities and time travel and multiple outcomes for my life. One imminent death if I don't go on a hunting trip and help this stranger find the missing key to the workings of the universe. But in the middle of the trip, I need to make sure I don't die. So go, but don't go. Don't not go, because he needs my help. But be careful. And figure out the dangerous places all on my own. But figure them out before I get there.

It's hypnotic and disturbing and addictive all at once.

For starters, who would do this to a person? Find a random stranger and tell her she's going to die. And then make up such a ridiculous *Quantum Leap* style story about it. It's not threatening, his voice. More reassuring. And smooth. Like if I met him in real life, he might be a friend. That's the scary part. That I think I'm trusting what he's saying. He might be hypnotising me like Paul McKenna. But I keep listening, hoping that it will finally make sense. Or just keep my mind so occupied that I don't think about the current fuck fuck-up that's my life.

When the batteries die and I'm not listening to anything, I keep the headset firmly in place so Mum and Dad won't try to talk to me.

The tape guy, Liam, is pretty crazy. Or super smart, I'm not sure.

He knows a lot about physics and wormholes, or so he says. I don't know how to figure out if what he is saying is true.

It's probably not. He said he's from the future. But not just the future, the future of another reality. So, if that's true, then what does it matter if I listen to him? Because what he says doesn't happen here, in this reality. Right?

It's confusing.

Basically, he says I go off on holiday and die. And then Michael's wife dies. But comes back to life. Then Michael's friend dies. But If I figure out some physics things with him here, then before I die, I can stop myself from dying and save Michael's friend too, and come back to a reality where he's never met me. Told you it was confusing.

But it won't happen for like another seven years, so I have time to figure it out. But time is also running out, 'cause it's a lot of work.

Whatever. Maybe I should listen to the tape again and take some notes. Maybe go to the library and see if there are some books that can help me out. Or heck, I should just go to the police and get them to find the guy. Oooh, a private detective could help. That would be exciting. But I don't think they would take me seriously walking in there with this as evidence. All I know is the guy is Liam, an American, and visited England once when he was a kid. That's it.

Actually, his dad is involved in physics too. And he says he knows Michael in the future. Hell, I really need to take notes next time I listen.

21

Christmas Eve used to be a great time for the Knights. Mike, Dad, and I would spend the morning eating and making sure the house had enough tinsel hanging from the ceiling.

Dad and I are getting food ready for Mike coming from the bus station, and Mum is pottering around, stressing whilst doing nothing. She's nervous. I'm enjoying it a little too much.

I keep looking at her from the corner of my eye, and she knows I'm watching her. It's the first time all week I've been in the room with both parents, minus my Walkman. And it's making her sweat.

Right on cue, Mike opens the front door. 'I'm here.'

Mum rushes from the kitchen at the back of the house to greet him.

When Dad and I join them in the hall, Mum rushes Mike through to the back and gets him settled at the kitchen table.

'You must be hungry.' Mum makes a plate of food for Mike and places it in front of him, not noticing that she's unintentionally taking the glory for making him his favourite fry-up. Maybe it's not unintentional.

Dad brings a pot of tea to the table and hands me an empty plate. We exchange glances as we fill our breakfast plates and I add two slices of white bread toast to the top and sit next to Mike.

'Don't sit down, dear,' Mum tells Dad over her shoulder. 'I need you and Caitlyn to go to the butcher's and collect the turkey. The queues will get too big if you wait any longer.'

Ever the dutiful dad, he stands up, makes his breakfast into a sandwich to bring with him, and downs a cuppa tea like its last orders in the pub.

I scoff and grit my teeth.

'Don't be annoying,' Mike tosses at me. He's being harmless, slipping back into his big brother role. 'Go help Dad,'

22

he says. 'I'll help Mum clean up here and get started on tomorrow's food.' He chews on some sausage and turns to Mum. 'You've been busy as usual. Make a list of any DIY things you need done while I'm here and I can help Dad out. In fact'— he points a fork at me—'you can help instead. It's about time you learn some carpentry jobs.'

I stare at them both and Mum shifts in her seat. There's fear in her eyes. 'Caitlyn has a lot of schoolwork to do over the holidays. She deserves a rest. She's been helping.' She pats Mike's arm.

She doesn't want us to spend time together in case I spill her secret.

Mum takes a gulp and tries to keep herself from falling apart. She dabs at her eye with her finger and tries to play it off as a scratch.

Mike mistakes her tears and nervousness as grief. He hasn't seen us much since Grandad died, so it's still new for him each time he comes home.

Mike snaps at me on Christmas evening when I don't sit with them to watch TV and play cards, and I don't see him again when he leaves early on Boxing Day morning. A reminder that my family is more broken than I ever knew. We're all just in survival mode. Work and sleep and get up the next day to keep it going. Only, my survival might be more of a literal thing.

The next week is spent remaking all the rooms and deep cleaning the kitchen and bathrooms for the January bookings. Mum was right. I have homework, but the excuse of working is way better than studying. I listen to the tape that Liam has recorded and take notes of the important lines I think

I should pay attention to. I never appreciated the music breaks he gives me right after a lot of information.

Music intervals, he calls them. To de-stress and absorb the things I'm learning.

I know the information I'm giving you is all heavy and out of this world, literally. But there was a fun element to recording this. I got to look up music from the '90s and remember some of my old favourites that you might know. Most are British music, because let's face it, British music is the best in the industry. But there are a few American tracks in here that I hope you like, even if you've never heard of them before.

Take a moment. Breathe and relax. This one is a classic.

'Let it be', by the Beatles, was the first break he gave me. It was the thing I needed to hear that first evening I fell asleep in the fortune teller's hut. Ironic, right?

But most of the songs he chose and recorded for me have become my favourites. I'm not sure if he chose them completely because he liked them, or because somehow, he knew I would love them, but I do. I've listened on the radio for them. I've re-recorded them on their own tape so I can listen on the way to school. But it's when I hear *Tupac* on the radio, a brand-new, only released today track, 'California', that I know something futuristic really is happening.

I've been listening to that song for the full month of December, and according to Natalie, the tape was in her possession for weeks before then. Which means Liam had this song, recorded and ready for me to listen to, before it was even released.

I'm sure it's possible the song has been in American studio hands for a while before today. Of course, it has. Buy why would anyone who had access to it spend their time messing with me?

24

When I rush home, I pull out the tape of music I have recorded of Liam's tracks and play and fast forward each one. Some he mentions by name, some only by the artist. Others I found on my own, or already knew them, so I have a pretty comprehensive list. I take off to the record store to see if I can find the others. In truth, I'm just looking for something else unexplained, like unreleased music, to make the person I'm building Liam up to be that little bit more real.

When I stand in line in the shop, I fiddle with the buttons on my Walkman, getting the music ready to play to the guy. There are only three more tracks that I don't know and have no idea how to find.

All I need to see is if any of these are from the future. If they are already released or the guy behind the desk knows about them, then I can score them off, too.

Private detective, here I come.

I've been here loads, finding new bands like Green Day that Liam has introduced me to.

'The first one I have,' the guy working the counter tells me. He pulls a REM CD album off the wall and places it on the counter like I'm going to buy it. 'Don't think we have that on cassette, though.' He types into the computer to check.

'And do you know the other two?'

He shakes his head. 'Doesn't ring any bells. Let me ask someone.' He waves over a girl working at the back of the store and hands her my headphones. She doesn't ask questions. They must get this a lot. She adjusts to the beat of the song and I'm a little disappointed that she might recognise it. I think I'm here more to prove Liam right than to find proof that he's a liar.

'No.' She shakes her head after a few minutes. 'Don't know either of them. But the second track sounded like Tupac singing, don't you think?'

'Yes!' The guy bangs on the counter. 'I knew it had a vibe about it. Let me listen again.'

They chat back and forth, trying to figure out what song it is, and keep asking which radio I recorded it from, or if I copied it from a friend to ask them. He has a computer that he can look up all songs and albums in the UK and USA for customer orders, but after trying new releases due soon, nothing seems to match.

When I step outside the store, I button up my coat and hitch my bag higher on my arm. The door to the music store bangs off my back as more people enter and exit, and I shuffle out of the way.

There's still a festive feeling in the air, with the dark evenings and the Christmas lights on proud display in the high street. It's nice. I used to love Christmas time. Despite never getting as many presents as some girls in school, I loved the fact that the whole family would have a few days together. With no B&B bookings over the Christmas week, Grandad would shut the cabin up and everyone would forget about work and real life for a while.

It was actually fun cooking with Mike. Even though we got the crappy job of prepping the vegetable and clearing up the peelings. Mum would stockpile some pineapple juice from the customers' bar area and let us make up weird and mostly disgusting drinks.

Christmas is going to be different now. Grandad is dead and Mike's moved away. Even though he came home, it wasn't the same. And it shouldn't be. Because apparently, we were never a happy family to start with.

I walk down the main street with a destination in mind and stand a little taller on my way. Walking with confidence, I'm more determined that the nothing I found in the music store is actually something. Nothing means it's still all a possibility.

It's all a riddle, really. Maybe that's a metaphor for my life. Or an omen. The only thing left for me to figure out is the wonders of the universe. Time travel and black holes and alternative realities. I'll need to find my library card. It won't open unit after the new year, so I'll have some time to figure out what to look for first.

I push the door to the off-licence open and grab a two-litre bottle of cider from the bottom shelf near the door.

Setting it on the counter, I look for some change in my pocket, trying to have confidence that I'm over eighteen and don't need to think about ID.

'ID?' the guy asks right on cue.

'I don't have it on me.' I shrug. 'Just finished work. You know how manic the Christmas shoppers are.' I chuckle slightly. One shop worker to another, right?

The guy doesn't look entirely convinced, but he also doesn't look like he entirely cares either. 'Bring it next time, okay?' He punches the prices into the till and I hand him the coins.

Cider safely packed into a blue plastic bag and I'm out the door, swinging my schoolbag around so I can hide the bottle inside. No need to get spotted by one of my friends' parents. I look up and see George standing in front of me. He's stalled short, like he saw me a few seconds ago and didn't know whether to keep walking past or stop and say hello. I look him in the eye while I turn and walk away.

CHAPTER

FOUR

CAITLYN RV 1:0
CAITLYN IS 16

I feel unsteady on my feet, like I've been travelling for too long. My inner ear feels blocked and I'm tired. I can feel myself sway slightly from side to side, like I've just got off a boat, and my body has yet to be told I'm on stationery land. I open the door in front of me, an old cabin door that looks like it could blow down with a good gust of wind, and I jump when I hear the bang of party poppers go off inside. A surprise.

A party for whom, I'm not sure, but the face before me seems to avoid eye contact. They are looking at the person behind me, trying to convey a secret message, maybe?

My attention is on the woman front and centre, who barrels past me and jumps into the arms of the waiting man behind me.

It's the feeling of disgust I recognise. The betrayal and annoyance of an affair I can't shake from my inward screams. I became my mother. A liar and cheater, and I hate myself more than I've ever hated her. I turn around and take small, tentative

*steps outside to the back of the hotel. I realise it was a hotel,
and I run. Just like I always do, I run away from the feelings.*

It's been a week since I met George on the street, and
I've had the same dream every night. I'm ready to move on, but
my mind isn't letting it go. I avoid bumping into my next-door
neighbour, which in itself is a miracle, since I used to see him
about four times a day. I lean over the side of the bed and puke
into my bin.

I always wake from these dreams hot and sweaty and
smelling something burning at the back of my nose. Like my
entire body wants to be turned inside out. But realising why
George was always in our house, or hanging around gardening
in the front, chatting over the stone bedding, is too much for
me when I already feel like crap.

I kick the covers off me and take the bin to the
bathroom to rinse it out. I'm ready to start a new chapter of my
life. New year's resolution and all that. Be better. Do better.
Live better. I'll be seventeen soon and finished school finally.
No more exams. No more teachers and people telling me what
to do.

Except, of course, this crazy project I've taken on to
follow what some stranger is telling me to do.

The local library is small, and the heavy shelves are
squeezed together. You can walk down them and look over the
titles of the books you want, but if you meet someone else
browsing, you both need to turn sideways to pass each other.
Most of the books are well old, and some of the ripped covers
are taped back together. It's not the most glamourous place to
be conducting grown-up research for my new adult life, but the
woman who works there, Lindsay, is helpful. She's younger
than you might imagine and has long black hair and studs on
her arms as bracelets, and she knew the title of the Greenday

29

album I wanted to order for a loan. If she had pink streaks in her hair, she would literally be my hero.

I was planning on looking for some books on the universe and time travel and wormholes that Liam told me to learn and research. But I think I want to learn about him too.

He said his first encounter with time travel happened in the early '90s on a trip to Blackpool, England, with his parents. This town is small enough that someone might just remember something.

Lindsay teaches me about microfiche and how to look up the past newspaper reports, and I start with the Blackpool news. Liam said he went missing during a trip, not for long, though, only half an hour or so, so I'm not really expecting it to be in the paper. But a lot of tourists get photos taken and write-ups in the paper for all sorts, so I'm looking for anything that might involve a tourist called Liam.

The library is quiet today, no teenagers studying and whispered voices carrying through the room. Only one old guy sitting in the reading chair with a newspaper. It's calming to have silence wrap around you. It's only the tick of the clock hanging behind the check-out desk that lets me know I've not fallen asleep.

It's three hours into the reading, and I have zero notes scribbled in my notepad, when Lindsay drops off a can of Fanta for me and whispers, 'Don't tell anyone I gave you this. And don't spill it.'

'Can I ask you where else I could find information?' I pop the top of the can and take a deep drink. The lack of windows makes it hard to judge the time of day, and suddenly I realise how someone could spend all day tucked up in a library. I'm parched, and as I drink, I realise I'm also starving.

She shakes her head. 'The only places to get the gossip is here or the pub. And you're too young to drink.'

The best thing about British pubs, or so the tourists tell me, is that kids and teenagers can go in for dinner. As long as they're not drinking, of course. A pub in America apparently is just full of people who want to drink. But I guess that makes us more sophisticated, that mostly we go for lunch or dinner and drink while we're there. Right?

The smell of beer hits the back of my throat the moment I cross the threshold, and memories of my cider hangover make me want to purge the smell and taste right out of me.

The Johnston family have owned the pub opposite Blackpool tower for three generations. Inside, it takes a second for my eyes to adjust to the dullness. The wood panelling is old, but instead of replacing it or—Craig is the grandson who is now older that my dad and in charge of the place—hangs up framed pictures of local points of interest.

People have donated things over the years, and Craig happily takes old relics as apologies for broken glasses and owed tabs from the locals.

Old, flowery teacups and saucers are pinned to the wall, American baseball caps, shovels and farming equipment that are apparently 'special' all decorate the walls. There is one wall covered in different beer mats that the barman made when he was on a quiet shift. It gets added to every year, and it has the most photos taken by tourists.

The noise of chatter doesn't die down, and I look for Craig, who works every day.

I move to the right-hand side of the pub, towards the restaurant area, and wait at the bar. My fingers land on the stack of plastic menus and I finger the side of the laminate while I wait. The smell of food is stronger here, covering up the alcohol and bad memories.

Chips, covered with vinegar, leave the kitchen, and my stomach rumbles when the waitress passes me. I never could resist the smell of vinegar. Mike was all about the tomato sauce when we were growing up. Splatted the red sauce all over every meal. But for me it was the salt and vinegar that I loved. Just like Grandad. He would even add salt to the chip butty a bite at a time. Maybe that's what caused the heart attack. Another memory, now tainted with death and destruction.

We're not the happy family we once were. And I never want to sit and pretend again that our lives are picture-perfect. Mum always wanted people on the outside to think that there were no problems. No unpaid bills or fights in the middle of the night. But I'm sick of plastering on a fake smile and pretending. Turns out her lies weren't just for those on the outside.

Craig's pulling a pint and shouting an order to one waitress to clear a table near the back, when I catch his eye. 'Any chance of a quick question?'

'Sure, love, what do you need? Not a job. I'm already fully staffed for the winter.'

'No, I just want to ask about a kid who went missing here.'

''Aint no kids ever went missing from here, love. Not that I know of.'

'No.' I shake my head. 'He was only missing for half an hour, but apparently his parents went crazy trying to find him? I'm not sure when it was. It could have been years ago. Or last year. Maybe?'

Liam said it was years ago, when he was a kid. But how old is he now? Or in the future when he made the tapes? I actually have no idea if he is even born yet. Maybe none of this

32

has happened to him yet. Heck, he could also be an old man. But I don't think he sounds like an old man. He sounds like a young, good-looking guy. I scold myself. How the heck could I figure out if he's good-looking from a voice? Even though it sounds like the nicest, smoothest voice I've ever heard. Doesn't mean he's as hot as I hope he is.

A voice in front of me pulls my eyesight back into focus and what's happening right in front of me.

'Ah, a lost kid, happens all the time.' Craig hands the guy at the bar his change. 'Hard to keep track of in the summer. Why? What's so special about this one?'

'Nothing, I guess. Just someone was telling me a story, and I wanted to check it out. I'm not even sure when it was. Just the family was American, and the boy was called Liam? Ring any bells?'

Craig tilts his head. 'There was one American family that caused a ruckus a few years back. The boy was a bit dazed when they found him, said he hadn't left, and was screaming about lights and stuff. Epileptic fit or something. Had to call an ambulance. Is that what you were talking about?'

'Maybe. Did you get the family name?'

'No.' He shakes his head. 'They were staying round the corner. If I recall. Stayed longer than planned as the kid was admitted to the psych ward for a couple of days. Up in arms the parents were. Not sure if he had been assaulted or abducted by aliens.' Craig chuckled.

'Which B&B were they in?'

'Your neighbour George's. He might have the family name if you ask him.'

Fan-fucking-tastic.

33

One thing is for sure, I'm not going to George for any favours.

I asked Natalie if she could see if her uncle had any visitor books from a few years ago, but she was asking too many questions about why I wanted to know, so I let it go.

The day before Michael's birthday, Mum is making her usual chocolate cake and tells me we're driving to Cambridge to meet him.

And just when I vowed off fake family lunches. It's all right. I can ignore her in the car with my Walkman, just as much as I can at home.

With the four-hour round-trip drive, plus lunch, I better pack some spare batteries. I know before checking there won't be any in the kitchen drawer.

I run upstairs and grab my purse, counting out the coins I've collected over the last few weeks. Some change, left in a room after check-out, and a pound that someone tipped me when they left is all I have to my name. Even pocket money from Mum and Dad doesn't come every week like it used to.

The newsagents at the end of the road is the closest thing we have that isn't a tourist souvenir shop. It's also expensive compared to the supermarket, but I don't have the time or the bus fare to get out there.

The shop is part of a house that faces the main front at the edge of the pier. It's small and crammed with everything you might need. Bread and milk and sweets, and random things that you never knew you needed until you see them hanging from a plastic strip at the edge of a shelf. I'm in luck and they stock small packs of batteries, so I don't have to buy a family pack. When I get to the counter, I see a *staff wanted* sign at the tills.

When the shopkeeper rings up my stuff, I'm still staring at the sign.

34

'Can I have a job?' I blurt out.

Embarrassment covers me all over, heat creaking into my cheeks and running the entire way down my chest. I can feel the prickles move along me. I know for sure that's not the most professional way to apply for a job, but hey, I've done it now. I keep my head held up high and wait for him to answer.

'Aren't you the Knight kid? You already have a job at the B&B, don't you?'

'I need a paid job,' I tell him.

He nods in understanding, and I know this is my opening. I tell him about all the things I do at the bed-and-breakfast, and all the jobs and responsibility and customer satisfaction. I let him know that I'm still in school, but after four o'clock and homework and the B&B, I could do a couple of hours at night, or on the weekends. He halts my blabbering with a hand in the air.

'I don't need help here at the shop. It's my son. He opened a car wash off main street, next to the amusement slots. Real busy on the weekends. Be there at eight a.m. Saturday and I'll let him know I already hired you.'

I can't hide my smile when I thank him, but I control the little hop and jump that's dying to bounce out of me, and I carefully and gracefully walk out the door. I don't even know how much I'm getting paid, but I don't give a damn. I'm going to work my ass off and have enough money to go find Liam and this stupid universal time travel hole thingy.

If you've ever been excited and nervous, you'll understand the feeling of sickness in your throat and butterflies in your belly.

You wish it would all be over with, so the feeling would go away, but the excitement is real and infectious and you want to jump up and down and show the world what's happening.

That's how I feel.

It's a dream.

I know it's a dream because I'm older and somewhere in the sun.

I'm dressed a little like grunge-librarian Lindsay, with black hair dye and streaks of green through it, big, chunky boots and short denim shorts with a tank top. I feel I'm on holiday, with the sun beating down on my back, so hot I can feel the drops of sweat beading. And the happy feeling running through my veins. I've just found something really important. Some information. Some secret wisdom that makes dream-me thrilled. And the guy I'm with happy too.

The guy takes my hand and squeezes it tight as we walk back to a Jeep. I look down at his hand and see a wedding ring on my finger. When he sees me staring, he twirls the ring around my finger and speaks in a familiar American accent. 'It takes some getting used to, right?'

I jolt awake in the back seat of the car, Mum and Dad up front driving the two hundred miles back home from meeting Mike in Cambridge. When I jerk up, Mum turns from the passenger seat.

'You have a bad dream?' she asks.

I flop back into the seat, loosening the seat belt around my shoulder, and take a deep breath. What the fuck was that?

Grandad taught me a lot about psychology. He said it was the best tool he had in his industry, to know how people operate. Natalie still teaches me a few things here and there. I know my dream wasn't about Liam, per se, but about someone I think he might be. That I've been obsessing over him for months, have listened to his voice for hours on end, it is buried deep in my subconscious and I'm able to replicate it in a dream. But it felt like it might have been him.

I'm not sure what he really looked like. I never looked at his face long enough in the dream, and when I glanced up, the sun was shining down on my eyes, making him appear more like a silhouette. His hair must be long as it was tied back in a bun, more like a girl's, but it looked cool. I've never seen a guy with hair that long before. He must be confident to pull it off, or maybe in the future, all guys are confident. But his hands were pretty. Can someone even have pretty hands? They fit nicely around mine, and they were warm and caring when he squeezed mine gently. He had tattoos over his arms, and I really wanted to see them all. I do like tattoos, so maybe I was just filling in the blanks with what I want him to look like.

My official diagnosis of myself is that I'm becoming obsessed with a guy I've never met.

Great.

I think I need to talk to Natalie about what I should do. Despite fortune tellers getting an awful reputation, the good ones can actually give you loads of advice.

They're like trainers in the gym. They help you get to where you want to go, if you're too scared to go without a nudge in the right direction. That's what Granddad always said. Most people don't know how to shape or manifest the life they want, and they don't believe it's under their control. All he did was find out what they want and offer them a nudge toward the things they need to get them there. They make their own future.

But the real trick, the thing that gave Grandad and *Knight's fortune* a great reputation was his ability to figure out what people wanted without them telling him.

Finances, relationships, and grief. Those were the top three things that brought people to fortune tellers, he said.

Once you worked out which category they fell into, you could take it from there.

Basically, everyone wants to know their life will all work out. Grandad would get them to admit what their desires for the future were, and then give them the confidence to go get it. Once it came true, that was the winner right there.

For me, in these circumstances, he would tell me I'm chasing a boyfriend. That I want a relationship. That I'm grieving for my family. The death of my grandad, my brother moving away, and the possibility of my parents separating. And that all those things put us in a financially vulnerable position. That I've created a situation to concentrate on that guarantees my future. Something to focus on and chase down.

I do what my grandad taught me. I make a vision board. I took some old magazines from the guest sitting room and flip through them in the back seat. I realise I'm looking for two things. A new place to live and an adventure. Or heck, maybe a place to live out an adventure. I want to be anywhere but here. And I look for a guy with tattooed arms to be with me.

I can't find exactly what I'm looking for and switch to written form instead. I'm not sure what came first, my desires or Liam's tapes, but the more I write, the more I list similar things to what Liam says I should go look for.

This is what Grandad said about reading people's fortunes. Find the things they want and present them to them as a future possibility. If only they're brave enough to go chase it. Maybe Liam's just a really good tourist-fortune-teller and not a time-travelling, reality-bending stud. I'm sure he's a stud. He's American, right?

Based on Liam's tapes, I need to wait until I'm old enough to travel the world before I can go chasing the things he wants me to learn. It's not like my parents won't notice. If I go on a year-long backpacking vacation. At least it gives me time to save.

I understand now what Liam means by *having* time and it running out simultaneously. There's only so much that can be done now, and the rest is going to have to wait until the future. Go looking too early, and the things that I need might not even be in play yet. I'm waiting in limbo.

Abandoning the vision board and notes, I turn to a fresh page in my diary and write out instructions to myself from Liam.

From my research with David, it looks like there are many things that can affect time travel, and not just the physics. Being able to land in the right spot is something that is going to affect how far forward or backwards a person can go. Because not only will the subject have to move through time, but the space of the universe, too. Because of the earth's rotation around the sun, the earth itself is not always in the same physical space. If you jump time, you better make sure you have a harness to the location you are leaving or entering, because the last thing you want to do is send yourself off and the earth isn't there to catch you.

Anchorage is what you need to figure out. We think our previous time-travelling subject was anchored to another person. But that's only one theory. And it looks like the version of you that died wasn't anchored enough. So, we need to work on anchoring you to the earth. And an anchor works best when it's sunk the whole way to the bottom.

The earth's core.

In theory, it's the same distance wherever you are. But the best magnetic disruption often occurs along the equator. So maybe the centre of the earth is just volcanic substance, and it's the equator that will give us what we need. You're going to have to test that one yourself. See what you react to the most.

Notes:

1. Go to the equator.

2. Access the centre of the earth.

3. Look out for any quirky feelings.

Sounds simple enough. First part is getting enough flight money.

CHAPTER
FIVE

Where did I go wrong? I know there must have been something I didn't follow right or something I missed. I mean why the hell would Liam and the universe go to so much trouble to bring me here, to give me all this information from the future, just to see me die alone in a cave at the other end of the world?

CHAPTER

SIX

CAITLYN 1:0
1995
CAITLYN IS 16

The nightmares are getting worse. I sit up in bed and breathe slowly, trying to calm my heart. Dying in a cave has become a new fear.

I've never been near caves, but in my dreams, it's the most beautiful cave you could imagine. With blue and green swirly lights. I'm stuck there and I'm going to die. I have a bang to the head in my dream, so things are a little dizzy when I'm looking around, and even when I lie down and close my eyes, the dizziness doesn't go away. I just wake up in my bed, sweating and having heart palpitations.

Maybe I'm becoming claustrophobic. Grandad would've had a theory for me.

My bedroom door rushes open and Dad is standing there. 'Are you okay?' he asks.

Mum is hot on his heels. 'She's fine. Go back to bed. It's still early,' Mum answers for me. 'Did you have a nightmare?'

I shake my head at her, rather than her question, as she shoos Dad out of my room and sits on my bed.

I wait until I hear the creak of their bed as Dad climbs back in.

'Are you going to keep everyone in this family away from me so I don't spill your secrets?' I ask her as I lie down on my side, not waiting for an answer, merely an acknowledgement that she won't leave me alone with Dad or Mike in case I find the time to open up to them.

Mum pats my leg over the duvet. 'You can't tear us apart like this,' she whispers. 'He'll never get over it. It's done now, me and George. No point in upsetting everything for something that's over.' There is a shake in her voice.

'Shut my door on your way out,' I tell her.

I open up my Walkman to listen to the B side of the tape before I get out of bed. This side is the most specific, and the most vague one, I've decided.

I throw my duvet to the side of the bed and lean out, stretching towards my schoolbag that I dumped against the wall when I came home last night. Inside the bag, I push aside homework books and my pencil case and let my fingers scrape the bottom of the bag. There is a second cassette, bound inside the elastic band next to the original one.

My attention is on full alert, and I leap from the bed, sinking down into the carpet. Using my bed as a backrest, I stare at the tapes, like they might multiply even more right in front of my eyes.

I untangle the rubber band and slide the two tapes apart. The newer one—still looks old and beat up—but the plastic casing isn't cracked the way the first one is. This label is red, not blue. Which, my detective skills tell me, means Liam never bought them in a multipack. There were different tapes he's found lying around and re-recorded over them.

I open up the cover and slide the tape out, being extra cautious with the brown exposed taping at the bottom. I've never damaged a cassette before, but I should take more care of this one. Maybe I'll re-record them onto spare tapes.

43

In the same handwriting, scrawled in the middle of the lines is:

YOU'RE NOT LISTENING TO ME.

The tape is rewound and ready to play on side A, so I slide it into the Walkman and put on my headphones.

Liam's voice fills my ears, and receiving new words from him feels like I've been given a reward. He's real, and he can speak more than the hour and a half I have imbedded in my brain.

So, apparently, you're not listening to me. Because I've not disappeared yet, and I still remember you as being dead.

I'm not sure if I'm mad that you're listening to the tapes but not really hearing what I'm saying, or if you're actually not listening to the tapes. Or maybe I'm not giving you as much as you need to make better decisions in all of this. Either way, clean out those ears and give me your full attention.

After my first brush with time travel, a traveller visited me and my dad. It was then that my dad started believing in me and started research in the field. Years later, David, the traveller, was younger and joined our team at the university.

You can imagine how hard that was for Dad and me, not to mention that we knew in the future he would travel to our past. That our project must have worked, that our research was proven.

In my reality, right now, David is in trouble. He is unconscious and we think he hasn't made it back from the time-travelling trip he took to me and others in the past. He died with us in the past, and now here, in 2016, in my present, we can't wake him up. But here's the real kicker.

You've been dead for years. I never met you. I only ever knew you as Mike's younger sister. But his wife, Audrey—she's travelled through time too—she says that's all wrong. That she's from a reality where you are alive and well. So things have got fucked up. People have crossed realities they're not supposed to. And I do not know which one you are. If you're the one who lived or died. But I've tried my best to get to where I need to go. To give you the information you need. That hopefully, whatever version you are, you can save yourself and David, too.

Anchorage, remember. David really is the smartest one of us all. Follow him, when you feel you're being pulled—follow him and save him.

After David died, his body disappeared from the morgue. Everyone thought it was the guy who murdered him, but I think it might have been you. I hope it was you, and me and us who are all trying to save him.

Don't be scared of the murderer. He was only ever after Stella. David just got in his way when he was protecting her. He always does that. In every reality. Love will do that to you— cross dimensions to keep each other safe.

My legs have goosebumps running up the back, all the way over my arse, and I feel both cold and sweaty. I clutch the Walkman to my chest and wait until the tape reaches the end and clicks off. There are no more words. Just half an hour of silence. He recorded nothing else. It was a warning about how I'm still going to die.

But the thing I focus on the most, the thing I never realised... I might be able to communicate with him.

By 9:00 a.m. on Saturday morning, my feet are soaking and my arms are sore. The car wash is harder work than it looks. Especially since everyone in Blackpool seems to get their car washed in the morning.

45

Crouching by the front wheel of car number twenty-three of the day, I rub the soapy cloth over the wheel trim like I was shown and leave the froth of soap heavy before I move on to the next one. I have to admit, the two boys who set up this business know exactly what they are doing. A disused lot at the back of their dad's shop, with added drainage and what can only be described as a broken old bus shelter to house their cleaning supplies and hoses. The cars are lined around the street, and for £2.50, who can blame them? We work fast, and in sections, always keeping the conveyor belt of cars moving through the space.

My hands are red with the cold, despite the water starting at a lukewarm temperature. It doesn't take long for the temperature to plummet in the winter by the sea.

I see Natalie's feet before she speaks and when I look up, she's holding a green pair of wellies and smiling. 'Thought you might need these.'

I jump up and grab them out of her hand. 'Oh my god, thank you!' I sigh. 'I'm literally in a puddle of water here.'

Natalie winks over at my new boss, Konnor. 'I got a call to come sort you out,' she says. Konnor nods at me and takes my place, while I step to the side and lean on Natalie to change into my new, dry wellies. She's also packed a bag with a towel, dry socks, and rubber washing up gloves. 'You really should have thought this through before you got hypothermia on your first day,' she says.

I nod. 'I've had a lot on my mind. I was up late getting the kitchen ready for this morning since I wouldn't be there to help with the breakfast shift.'

'What did your mum say about you working?'

'She was actually happy.' I shrug. 'I told her I wanted to save for college, and I think she realised it would be less time

46

for me to be around Dad, so she gets to sleep around a little longer.'

Natalie grimaces and lowers her eyes.

'Sorry,' I say. 'I know George is your uncle, but—'

'Don't apologise. What they did is unforgivable.'

'What they're doing.' I correct her, pushing my hands into the yellow rubber gloves and packing my wet shoes into the shopping bag she brought. 'I know they're still doing it, and I'm expected to keep my mouth shut. Well, it won't be long and I'll be out of here.'

I nod over her shoulder at the line of cars. 'Need to get back.'

'Come meet me at the beach tonight. Party at the side of the pier. Before this place erupts into tourist central again. We can talk properly about what's going on.'

'I don't want to talk about it,' I tell her with a smile. She is the only person who's ever there for me. Despite being too old to be my friend, and too young to be my mother, she fills both voids.

'I'm talking about your aura. There's a huge electric storm brewing around you. Something big is changing in your life, and I think you know what it is.'

After finishing work at 6:00 p.m., Konnor drives me home and I accept the lift despite only being a few minutes' walk around the corner. He tells me how he and Natalie went to school together, and I realise he's another local twenty-something who's running their own business. I used to feel bad for the people who never left town. But maybe generations of business management run in the blood here. Maybe it's not a terrible life after all. Ten hours of work and £35 in my pocket is more than I've ever had at once. Konnor tells me he'll set up my tax records by next week, but I shouldn't have much deductions. He's booked me into work every Saturday and explains about the valet services they fill on Fridays, and he's hoping to expand into during the week hours too.

'I have school and the B&B to work in,' I say. 'But Fridays after school would work, if you have the hours.'

'Sure thing.' He pulls over at the kerb. 'I might see you tonight. Natalie invited me to the beach too. It's been a while since I've seen the guys from school.'

'Are you and Natalie a thing?' I'm not sure why I ask him and not her.

Konnor goes red around his neck and tries to play it off. 'We were once. And I miss having her as my friend.' He looks at me. 'Why? Does she ever talk about me?'

I purse my lips. 'We don't really talk about guys. I'll see you at the beach.'

I go straight to my room and tentatively sit on the edge of my bed. My room is a mess and it bugs me. It also bugs me to clean it, so it's a lose-lose situation every day. I've fallen behind on the things I do for myself. My bed is unmade, and it makes it easier to lie on my side and throw the blanket across me for a bit of heat. Reaching out, I knock over a can of body spray, find the alarm button on my clock radio, and set it for 7:00 p.m. Enough time to get ready and go to the beach by eight. It's already dark out, and I'm still freezing, so I make plans to wear jeans and boots and dig out my coat from the downstairs cupboard behind the kitchen. I can spend £5 on a bottle of cider and a bag of chips for dinner on the way to the beach and still have a decent amount of savings from my wages today. The thought makes me smile and makes every aching bone in my body worth it. Step one of my life is moving into place. I already have a route planned for investigating this crazy new venture that's landed on me. And I have a legitimate way of getting there. And getting there prepared. Knowledge is everything, Liam said. Knowledge and preparation.

I found a course in university that will help me. Newcastle runs a degree in Portuguese and Spanish with Latin American studies. Combine that with French, which I'm doing at school, and I should be able to communicate in most of the countries along the equator. And my body is screaming at me that step four needs to be bumped up a bit. Fitness. The places I need to get to are going to be out of reach for the Caitlyn I currently am. I need to get fit and strong. Gym membership is way too expensive, but I checked out a fitness book from the library and combine that with jogging, and I should be able to get in much better shape. Newcastle University has a student gym and classes that are totally cheap. Hiking and rowing and even kickboxing. Honestly, I can't wait to get there.

Before my alarm even goes off, I have the energy to get out of bed and gather my things for a shower. I shove the clothes that are hanging half out the drawers away and push them closed to give the appearance of a tidy room. I hang up my dressing gown and pull the duvet straight on the bed, making it look a little like it's made. It's not the standard I have to do each day in the guest rooms, but it's enough for now.

My makeup bag is half empty over the table, along with homework notes and the growing pile of library books. I gather the makeup and nail polish and slide it all with a thump into the bottom of the bag. I feel a little better with the semi-tidiness now before me, and I head for the bathroom and relax under the hot spray of water. I can feel the heat in my bones, and even after I've dried off and dressed, and walking down the windy promenade towards the beach and the sound of music

49

and chatter, I'm on fire with the adrenaline of talking through my plan with Natalie.

I spot her and Konnor and a couple of others near the small firepit in the sand, and I make my way towards them. They must have been here for a while already, as there are discarded towels on the sand and a bag of rubbish near the music speaker. The scattered groups of people from school and others from town stretch from the steps all the way to the edge of the foaming sea to the driftwood and broken shells at the foot of the pavement, vary in age. Everyone keeps to their own little groups, and there's never any trouble. Small town and people try to keep to themselves as much as they can. Especially when you're sneaking around with a bottle of cider in your bag. Two girls are already twirling each other around in a ballroom dance, laughing as their bare feet sink into the sand and they stumble with their steps.

Natalie turns around as I approach and before I'm even with her, the sky opens up and the rain falls heavy and fast over the beach. People scream and gather their things as the fat drops of cold water descend upon us. I crunch my face up in disappointment at being soaked for the second time for the day while a roar of thunder cracks around the open seafront. The sound of crashing waves is drowned out by the unexpected storm, and the firepit is extinguished to a pile of smoking ash. Natalie grabs my hand and pulls me in for a hug while she screeches with laughter. We run across the beach to the pier for shelter. The wind and rain cause my hair to stick to my cheeks as we run, and the taste of salt coats my mouth. I can't help but laugh as we all scatter for cover.

Before we get far, a crack of lightning strikes and the strength hits in my veins as we're knocked off our feet.

People are running towards us. I manage to partially sit up, leaning on my arm to try and look around for Natalie. She's

50

lying next to me and when people reach us, they stop and stare.

'Jesus,' Konnor says. 'Are you okay?' He bends down to check on Natalie.

There is a moan coming from her. She's alive and conscious, but if she feels like me, it will feel like a truck hit her. Konnor helps her to her feet. Something falls from her pocket and I grab it for her while we get steady on our feet.

When I reach for her, Natalie pulls back. 'Don't touch me.' She shrugs away from my reach. 'You're dangerous when the lightning comes.'

'What the hell does that mean?' She can't think I made the lightning strike her, right?

'Stay away from people when the storms are brewing.' She looks at me like she's scared of me.

Konnor helps Natalie along the beach, out of the rain. The three of us take tentative steps off the beach to the road.

He turns back to me, whispering, 'She doesn't know what she's saying. Don't take it personally.' Konnor is holding a lot of Natalie's weight, and I wonder how she's so much worse off than I am. I open the folded card that fell from Natalie's pocket and see that it's a red tarot card. I fold it back up and put it in my pocket. She'll want it when she's better.

Someone must have called for help, as a car pulls up to take us to hospital.

Konnor loads Natalie into the back seat and he motions for me to climb in. I shake my head. 'I'm fine. I don't want to go.'

'Don't be stupid,' Konnor says. 'You got hit by lightning. You should be dead. Get in the bloody car.'

I take off at a run through the rain, back home. When I get into the safety of my room, I strip off my soaking clothes. It takes a few minutes to push the wet jeans down my legs, and

51

my underwear rolls down with them, clinging to the fabric like glue. My socks hang halfway off my toes, and an ache has started in my bones that means I don't want to bend down and take them off completely.

In front of the mirror, I turn to look at the marks on my back, lifting my jumper up and over my head, T-shirt too, so I stand there in just my bra.

My body is red and splotchy from the cold, but the blue marks that highlight what looks like burning in my veins is so weird that I stare at it for ages.

What the hell? It's not sore, but my back and legs ache from where I landed in the sand. I grab my pyjamas and throw them on, not caring for a shower. I just want to get into the bed and heat up. I pull the tarot card out of the back of my jeans to let it dry. Unfolding it, I look closer at the bolt of lightning cracking right through the centre of the card. My heart stops.

I look at the card more carefully. Three people falling from the sky around the lightning is depicted, right next to a tree on fire from the strike.

The phone downstairs rings, and I hear footsteps as my mum answers, then calls for me. 'Natalie's on the phone.'

I throw the blankets off. God, I hope she doesn't tell my mum I need to go to hospital. I'll never hear the end of how she's so worried about me. She does that, makes all accidents and stories about her. About how she's so worried and about how she's so tired sitting up in the hospital all night with me.

I run down the stairs, and apparently my legs aren't that sore, as I make it to the handset that my mum has abandoned on the phone console. 'Natalie? Are you all right?' I ask.

'I'm fine.' Her voice is quiet and shaky on the other end. 'What about you?'

'I'm okay. I think you got the worst of it.' I'm nervous to ask what she meant on the beach. If she really thought I was the one who hurt her. 'Did you bang your head when you landed?'

'I'm not sure. Konnor is checking me in. I just wanted to call you first. I'm not crazy, Caitlyn.' She talks fast. 'I know that everyone in this town thinks I'm crazy for believing in my abilities. But I'm not. You're dangerous, Caitlyn, and the sooner you see that, the sooner you'll be safe.'

'Natalie.' I gasp. 'You can't mean that. Look, I have the tarot card that fell from your pocket and it doesn't mean anything. It was a coincidence. Those things are a load of rubbish and you know it.'

I hear Konnor on the other side of the phone. 'Natalie, the nurse wants to see you. Hang up.' His tone is curt.

'Natalie, tell me you don't mean what you said.'

'Of course I mean it. And if you don't believe in me, then I can't keep helping you. You've taken too much already,' Natalie says. 'Stay out of my life.' The phone slams down on the other end, and I don't know if it was Natalie's anger or Konnor's frustration that ended the call.

PART TWO:

THE MIDDLE.
FORWARDS OR BACKWARDS—THE MIDDLE ALWAYS REMAINS.

CHAPTER
SEVEN

I never thought I would become a snobby traveller, but a seven-hour business class flight is much easier than economy. The seats are almost double the size, and I only had one other passenger next to me whom I ignored the entire trip. The leather seat that could be mistaken for an armchair reclined the entire way back, and the flight attendants were fussing over everyone with blankets and drinks. I never once had an uncomfortable moment on the plane. Mike originally booked me a first-class ticket, but the price difference was insane. I had no qualms about cashing it in for business class and flight credit for the next leg of this research trip. Technically, I'm saving him money, since he said he would pay for my travel and accommodation while I was out here. *Gallivanting around the world.* Mike calls it. But it's life or death, right? And it's about time I did something solid about saving my own life.

Working as my brother's assistant for the last two years in L.A. was both lucrative and boring. Who knew there were so many mundane jobs that needed doing for people who worked an eighty-hour week?

Moving from a small town to a big American city was amazing, and the weather and people were great. But I felt like I had traded one ordinary life for another.

I spent every evening out in the town and at bars and nightclubs, hoping to bump into anyone with the name Liam. Tattooed hunks were the first to grab my attention, but they never quite had his smooth voice, or the right tattoos I dreamed of. I don't know if Liam actually had any tattoos, but in my dreams, he did. And I can't help holding onto the idea that it might exist. But three one-night stands, a crappy bunch of dates with some other guys, and six questionable tattoos of my own, and I knew I was chasing a man who didn't exist.

No one can be that perfect.

Even if Liam is real, I know nothing about him. He's never going to be the person I think he is.

I let my head bang off the window with a thud as I look at the view coming in for landing. Deep, slow breaths. I can't get my lungs full these days. There's always something on my mind that makes it hard to breathe. And I'm aware of how spoiled that sounds sitting in my business class, round-the-world plane seat that my brother paid for.

When the plane touches the tarmac and bounces on landing, my giddiness turns up a notch. I'm finally here.

I've been dreaming of making a step in the real-life research work for so long that I never thought I'd actually be travelling. Miles away from Blackpool and parents who hate each other. I know when the plane door opens, the rest of my life will be waiting for me out there.

Even if I only have a short time left.

I'm only one week into my trip, and I feel excited and scared, the way I felt in my claustrophobic dreams. It's been seven years since I found the cassette tape in Grandad's hut. You would think I would be excited to be here, and I am. But there's a voice screaming in the back of my head that I don't need to do this ridiculous trip.

That maybe Liam isn't real after all. Years of chasing a ghost on tape have got me nowhere. Ecuador was the first stop on my list of locations, but there are so many places to see and people to talk to that the first week was spent finding my feet and got caught up on being a regular tourist. With nothing pulling at my inner anchor or instinct or whatever, the doubts crept in.

Sure, he knew my brother's name was Mike and that he had a friend David, but he could have found that out before he recorded the tapes. They were already at university together for like an entire year by that point. Moving to America and meeting a friend called Stella was the only thing so far that felt weird. Not entirely a coincidence. But hey, Mike always wanted to be an actor, and there must be loads of Stellas in America, right?

It's in the moments of fear like this that I try to rationalise everything.

The tour left this morning from the hotel in Ecuador to the deep caves, and now that I'm here, I can't help but think that this is the place of my dreams. Where I have my panic attacks and die.

But damn if I'm going to stick around. I don't even want to be here with the tour trip. But it's only an hour down the cave pathway, look around the natural light pool and back out, before the group needs to be on the road for lunch at the next village.

I can do this. I can survive an hour.

The walk down the cobbles and stones is unsteady, and I'm glad the tour insisted on sensible walking shoes. Not that I have much else packed. I knew I would do a lot of walking and hiking, so it's all I have.

These places seem so familiar to me, but I've been looking online for ages at all the places I needed and wanted to visit in person that everything feels like déjà vu.

The cave itself is a ten-minute trek from the road, so we are already walking at a good pace when we approach the mouth opening. The forest is stretched thin. We can still hear the traffic from the road we parked on. The mouth of the cave is low, and the guide crouches down and lets every one of us pass him while he repeatedly says, *mind your head*. But once we are two steps in, we can stand straight.

The inside is immediately impressive, especially if, like most of us here, you've never been cave exploring. There are rock formations that look like icicles hanging from the roof, and some that land into thick boulders on the cave floor. I'm sure there is some explanation for this, that the guide is talking about, but I'm looking further into the mouth of the cave. With each step I'm taking, shuffling through the dead leaves that have blown in, I know I'm getting sucked deeper and deeper inside.

'Can you see any natural lights in here?' I ask. 'The brochure said that at certain times of the year, light formations can be seen deep in the cave, that's thought to come from a reflection of a natural pool of water.'

'People aren't allowed to go that deep into the caves anymore,' the guide, Marcus, says disposedly. 'We'll only be walking ten minutes in, and the lights you're talking about were only reported by explorers who have spent weeks trapped below on their expeditions.'

'Let's not be a lost tour group,' one of the American tourists says.

Marcus nods, and the older guy in charge, Emmanuel, speaks. 'Of course. We didn't even bring lunch with us, let alone food for weeks,' he jokes.

The rest of the twenty-minute exploration doesn't actually take us far in the cave at all. Only a few minutes are spent actually going deep, while the guide stops every so often to point out apparent phenoniums. All I can focus on is the deep mouth of the cave and the urge to go exploring. And the choking sensation telling me to run. Too many dreams of dying in a cave have me cautious.

I'm not finding out anything here that could help with Liam's theory or time travel or anything whatsoever. I know I need to be brave and maybe hang back and go a little deeper without the group. But maybe knowing when to walk away is something I need to learn, too. Trusting your instincts is something Grandad always spoke about. Maybe I need to trust that this one trip will not give me all the answers. Not everywhere I look is going to give me what I want. You would think that years of waiting and planning had taught me patience, but Liam always said that time would run out. Once I was actually making progress, things would move so quickly that I needed to be ready.

Twenty-sixteen is a long way away. If things haven't started yet, then I don't need to worry, right? If I can just get past the version of me that dies soon, this should be plain sailing, right?

I fall back a few steps, slowing my pace so I end up being at the back of the tour group. Pretending to be examining

59

the markings on the cave walls, I run my hands over the bumpy walls and tug on some roots creeping through the rocks. As the group move towards the way we descended, I move further back, to the area we never explored. I want to get a better look at the places the tourists don't go. I need to see the places people don't talk about.

Only a few steps into the darkness, keeping my hands running over the cave walls, and I'm in dangerous territory. I can hear the group behind me, and they are moving slowly, so I'm not going to get left behind if I hurry. I dig around my backpack and turn on my head torch. Placing it quickly over my head, it flattens my fringe.

The tree roots are replaced with what looks like claw marks on the walls, but they are so big and deep, they could be from old tree roots. That's what it must be. I turn around to check behind me and the tour guide lights can be seen bouncing off the floor and illuminating the passageway out. To my side are two tunnels that are so neat and round, they could be manmade. Dug out, and on closer inspection, travel down at a steep angle. I lean forward, and even for me, it would be a tight fit. Maybe they aren't manmade. Holding on to the top of the circular entranceway, the rock crumbles slightly under my hand, and I rub the dirt between my fingers. This part of the cave doesn't feel so solid. Like maybe we're so deep that the rocks turn to air and dust.

I hook one leg high over the mouth of the opening and test it'll hold my weight by putting pressure on my leg. Twisting around, I take a brave, or stupid, head and body-first shuffle into the hole. I can go a little further and still be able to call for help if I need it. The bottom half of my legs are still outside the opening, suspended in midair, when I can't shuffle anymore. The space is getting smaller. I look ahead, and the light from my torch only shows dust floating in the dense air and blackness behind it. However deep this is, it's not something I can explore on my own. The angle is too steep and going headfirst into the unknown is stupid. Even for me, and I came to terms with my early death a long time ago. It takes all my strength to push backwards, and I let out a tiny girl huff and scream at the energy it's taking. Me. Head of the rowing team for Newcastle University Girls division. I dig my fingers into a fissure on what can be called the floor of this tight tube and push backwards. I bang my head off the rock ceiling. I let out a dull scream at the thump that's vibrating through my skull and something grabs my ankles and pulls me under. Screaming, my entire body is moving at high speed, and the empty circular tube I was stuck in isn't as empty as I thought, as two small eyes reflect off the light on my head torch and I scream like I'm living a nightmare.

I land with a thump on the cave floor, back where I started, the tour guide's assistant cursing me out in Spanish. I take a deep breath and clear my head that I wasn't being sucked deep inside, but being rescued and pulled out.

I look up at the opening and a small brown nose and two piercing eyes belonging to a rat the size of a rabbit peek out of the opening before jumping and landing on my head. Screaming, I thrash, jump backwards, and let the vermin skitter for a way out.

I forgot that an hour's hike into a cave means an hour back. But after my escapade, the two guides are exchanging heated blasphemy in Spanish, and the walk back is more like a march, with no stops to admire the natural beauties we saw on the way in. The guides are trying to keep their voices low, not to upset the rest of the group, but I can hear them calling me a stupid tourist who doesn't respect nature and its environment. Hell, if only they knew.

I missed something in there. I was close, but not close enough to get what I need. Liam always said that I had to find the thing I feel the most compelled towards. The thing that feels like it's anchoring me deep to it, and damn, I felt it in that cave. Part of me wants to go further. To believe in him and go back for another look. But the claustrophobia, the idea of dying down there alone, stops those thoughts immediately. I can feel my heart palpitations starting. The ones that are normally in my dreams. The ones that cause the sweats and the adrenaline rush when I wake. But I'm not sleeping this time.

I rush to the bus. I jump up each step to expel some of the adrenaline and energy, and I pull my bag up from the floor. In my seat, I take out my Walkman, but instead of listening to Liam's voice, I pull out Liam's music and press play. I'll close my eyes, and when the tape is done, I should be sitting in a nice South American village for lunch. Saving the universe and time travel be damned. This time, I'm choosing myself. If it's really important, I'll double back at the end of all of this and look again. It's not like Mike won't be able to lend me the extra flight money. When the bus gets back on the rocky road, all I can hear is soothing tunes that have set me off to sleep for years, and I imagine being up close and personal to some swirling northern lights, deep inside a dark cave with no light reflection.

The sixty-year-old, tanned and wrinkled tour guide sits down at the table next to me. 'You speak good Spanish,' he tells me. 'And you're kind. I heard you ordering your lunch and talking with the waitress.'

I nod. 'I have a degree in Portuguese and Spanish.'

'Really?' The surprise in his voice matches his expression. 'Not a lot of Americans would spend the time to learn our language.'

'I'm English. And I can say the same for the British too.' I smile tightly at him.

'You're backpacking for a while? Yes?'

I stare at him, not wanting to commit to any of my plans with him.

'You want a job here? The tourists, they like it when one of their own is here to interpret for them. And sometimes the staff I have can't understand all the accents. It would be good for us to employ you.'

I turn in my seat and think for a second. 'I need a job, but I'm not cheap. I was a celebrity assistant in America,' I tell him. It was technically true. 'I'm used to working for people with high demands. I also speak French, and I can understand a little Somalian, although I've not held a conversation with a local yet. Along with my language skills, I can deal with demanding people. I can be valuable.'

'You are a people pleaser,' he tells me.

'I'm a people appeaser. There is a difference.'

'I'm not familiar with this word. But I want to put you in the week's tour groups and get you familiar with the route and the information we give. Then you can help.'

I bag up my trash and stand. 'My degree also covered Latin American studies. I'll have no problem catching up. But if you really want me to be useful, I can help you put together a better tour for your guests. More in-depth.'

'OK, England. You have a deal. But if I don't like your plans and you're not hardworking, you leave after one month.'

I hold my hand out to shake. 'Deal, Ecuador.'

'And no crazy stunts. You go where I tell you and stay away from danger. Understand?'

I nod. 'Definitely don't want to go near the danger.'

After we drop the tour back at the hotels and hostels, Emmanuel keeps me on the bus with him and in less than five minutes, we are parked at a small house with a large garden, next to a car and two motorbikes.

63

Emmanuel shows me around the back of the house, to the kitchen that he uses as an office, and introduces his wife and teenage son. Speaking in Spanish, he quickly cuts off what his son is about to say when Emmanuel explains I'm the new tour interpreter and can speak Spanish. Damn. I really like to know what people are saying about me when they don't think I can understand.

His wife, Isabela, ushers me to the table and fetches bread and water, while she finishes cooking their evening meal.

Emmanuel offers me a weekly wage and board package that he either thinks is fabulous, or he is a really good actor. It's hard to tell after being in L.A. for so long.

'Can I see where I'll sleep?'

Emmanuel shows me out back towards the driveway and motions towards the car.

He explains that his eldest daughter, Fernandina, runs a hostel for the young backpackers, and he'll plan for a room for me. It will be shared, but he'll try to get one of the smaller rooms with two or three local workers, so I can sleep better. 'No partying if it makes you late for work,' he tells me.

Why do I always find myself mixed with the families of self-made business people? For once, can't I just be the most successful person in the room? It seems like my whole life, I've been drowned out by people who just have their shit together and can make a business out of anything. And I literally mean anything. Mike makes millions of dollars *acting*, for god's sake.

I quickly work out that my wages here will cover my food, and with accommodation included, I can make it work. The place is nice and clean. There is a large, open recreational space out behind the check-in desk, and the rooms are little huts, lining the property border around the court style garden. They look quaint and well cared for. Towards the front, Emmanuel tells me, are the smaller rooms, with only one or two sets of bunk beds, and he will ask my daughter to set me up with her for a while to get settled in. We pass a full kitchen, decked out with steel shelves and appliances that look like it could fit twenty people cooking at once.

The room he shows me is more of a tiny apartment than a short-term hostel room. There is a set of bunk beds on the side wall, and a two-seater couch on the other. A small fridge is the only appliance in here, but there are shelves of plants and books and ornaments. Someone is trying to make a home here. One folding slide door leads to a cramped bathroom that has shelves for storage and a towel draped over the shower curtain.

It's going to be tight if two of us are sharing.

'Are you sure Fernandina won't mind having a roommate?' I ask.

'Not when I tell her I'll pay your rent. She loves making money off me.' He chuckles.

I won't have any wages spare to save, but I'll get to cover the day-to-day expenses while I'm on this part of the trip. The more I can explore with local advice, the better.

It's not just the physical location of the equator I need to visit. But study comes from folklore and stories from the people who live here. Their experiences and feel for a place can be more valuable than any book or college professor.

Superstitions and traditions can be routed in some form of experiences that might mean something in this supernatural search. And there's no better way to study a place than to live here for a while and notice the difference between myself.

'Okay, Ecuador. Let's check me out of my hotel and get my belongings.'

Quito is full of the usual tourist traps, which I'll be able to visit for free now. But in researching further tour opportunities with Emmanuel, I'll be able to ask loads of questions without raising suspicion. Ecuador has so many deep caves along the equator, it will be the closest I could possibly get to the core centre of the earth. Add in mine shafts and sea diving spots. I'm going to need more than a few months here.

Mike bought me a ridiculously expensive new internet phone, so I'll always have access to emails and online work if I need it, but so far, I've only been able to connect in the hotel business suite. Emmanuel knows one of the desk managers and explains I'll be working for him and need computer access to help set up new tours. He offers the manager a cut of the new tour sales price for help in setting up the research and advertising through the hotel lobby. The manager gives me a schedule of the quiet times that I can use their computers, which happens to be now, and Emmanuel leaves me for the evening. If I check out in the morning, I can get a refund for the unused week on my original booking. One last night of luxury won't hurt, right?

When I log into my email, there is an interpreter job offer from Stella, labelled *Just in case you need a job*. I smile inside and open up the email to the full screen.

The contract offer is to translate a novel into Spanish, and if the author is happy, a second job offer for French might also be available. Stella got first refusal through a publishing contact she uses for securing production rights. It pays so well, I can't even consider saying no.

It will give me something to focus on in my downtime. I need a solid distraction from the big stuff.

I download the book file onto my phone and let Stella know that I'll read it through first and let her know how long it will take for full translation.

Before I leave, I open up an old email I sent myself and print out the document I have there. A map and list of South America where the equator runs, as well as the islands to the west of the continent. Since Emmanuel is such a business guru, he might just be on board for a new business venture— widening his tour horizon beyond Quito and Ecuador.

One thing I learned from Mike and high value contract offers is you've got to move fast. I figure the easiest and best fit for me is to put together a business proposal on Equator Tours for Emmanuel.

I've listed all the thirteen countries that the equator moves through and done my research on tourists moving from country to country. It's going to take more time to make business plans for moving through each country, but I want to get Emmanuel on board now. The South American countries would be the easiest to start the expansion, so I've listed Ecuador, Columbia, and Brazil as phase one.

Once we have established the routes, points of interest, and folklore, we can test the long-haul route.

Pricing is something that Isabelle is going to have to work on, since she does the business accounts. But moving continents is going to be tricky. We might have to set up business partners or overseas staff to manage those. We can send the tourists on flights to pick up the next tour guide. Or heck, Emmanuel might want to franchise in the other countries. The first couple of tours will need Emmanuel and me to go along and make sure everything runs smoothly, but first I've got to convince him.

I gather up my proposal and the rest of my belongings and wait outside for Emmanuel to collect me. Always checking on my prized possession, I wind up my headset and place it in the bag, but when I push everything aside to get the headpiece in place without breaking it, I see a reflection of plastic. It's a new tape. I now have three. I've told myself these past years that the second tape must have always been in the brown envelope. That I just never saw it until those weeks later. But now this one has turned up, just as mysteriously. There's no way someone slipped the tape into my bag. And who the hell would play a con this long, anyway?

I load the new tape into the drawer. Like the last one, it's ready to play on side A.

'Don't go back,' is what Liam says. The tape goes on to briefly explain how Liam has no further information on the future of my life in the timeline I'm in. And how that brings with it its own dangers. There was a reason he never completed this part of the research so thoroughly. One was the time constraints it would put in other places, but the second was the sheer size and dangers along the equator line.

Just because we might get me past the age of twenty-four, where I died in his timeline, there are now a whole host of branches my reality can splinter off to. I managed to change the universe once. But death could be a consequence of every choice I make.

CHAPTER
EIGHT

2015
Caitlyn is 36

From the Galapagos Islands and across South America, I spent most of my time in this part of the world. Finding things I never knew I was looking for, as well as the clues to the universe that brought tropical lightning and cave diving to meet somewhere in the middle. Measuring energy levels in the air, the sea, and the sky. Working out how much is natural phenomena, combined with human energy and the right combination at the right time. Relying on the earth's rotations and the sun rising each day kept me on track to find the secrets of the universe. The things right in front of us that we just cannot see. The wonders of the light spectrum that our human eyes aren't privy to. The boiling of a thunderstorm—we've yet to figure out how the power of lightning begins. The power of the centre of the earth, the core of the world. Heat and power from deep within, spilling out of volcanoes, telling us that the world is a living, breathing organism of its own, and we are yet to understand how to even begin to harness any of its power. Because we are powerless. Unless...

Unless Mother Nature herself blesses you with her touch. With a stroke of her power, so you can see. See what others cannot. Do what others only dream of. What science is chasing and what people live for. Answers. Love. Family and belonging. Self-actualisation and becoming a wonder of the world.

I had it all, but the love was fake. And it broke me.

Crossing the equator on as much land as I could, I left my sweat and sometimes a little of my blood on the mountains. Bringing home blisters and dirt under my fingernails. Deep sea diving and cave exploring. Trekking through the rainforest. Exploring concave volcanos and manmade landmarks. Abandoned mineshafts and the stories surrounding them. Three thousand kilometres, in the tropical heat and dust, from one end of South America to the other.

My body changed over the years. The leg muscles that drove me one step in front of the other. The stronger back and core, that helped me drag my supplies on each trip and calm my breathing and heart rate with Pilates in the morning. Each day, setting my head in the right place so I could find what I was looking for while putting death in a neat pocket to deal with another day.

Sailing across Null Island and leaving my heart and sanity in Sao Tome and Principe. Central Africa became the place I rushed through, just to tick off the list of research bases. By this point in my life, I knew there was nothing left for me on this road, so to speak.

I had found all the folklore surrounding the smaller villages off the beaten track. I had spoken to fortune tellers and witches and healers. I had put my faith in every scrap of information I could find to bring it all back and see what fit. See what might be true and what might work in the world of time travel. It was all beginning to muddle. After the first four years, I was finding nothing new.

Settling down and starting a life was my first mistake. Trusting a guy with my business and my heart and my fucking sanity was the mistake that broke me.

Even crossing the equator through the Maldives didn't offer the reprieve or therapy I was looking for. Island hopping through Indonesia, I took on the spoiled tourist persona and spent my nights in hotels rather than camping and exploring like I should have been. I didn't miss swatting insects off me in the middle of the night, or securing my food away from the campsite in case animals came roaming in the middle of the night. I jumped on flights rather than boats. And I drank margaritas with dinner instead of evening jogs around the places I was stopped at.

Kiribati was the last stop, and I only managed a day there, most of it driving from and to the airport. I don't know why I bothered with the last four years of my life. I should have just gone home earlier. I should have called it quits or stayed in England on my one visit home since I left seventeen years ago.

Bloody hell, seventeen years since I've been in Blackpool. Mike was married in Ireland ten years ago in 2006 and I flew there from London, getting a consultant job with an author on the way. Three weeks back in the UK and I was literally itching under my skin to get back on a plane.

At least I'm going home to Mike in L.A. and not Blackpool. To the house I grew up in, that another man now lives in with my mum.

Dad says he doesn't care that she kept the B&B, that he's happy in the house Mike bought him, and he'd rather be fishing and taking life easy. But it still stings that my mum and George lost nothing. They gained each other and combined their two houses and two businesses.

I should be happy for her. But it still smarts every time I remember the secrets she made me keep. The betrayal she made me a part of. It must have seeped into my blood because how else would I end up in the same position all these years later?

71

My backpack dangles at my feet as I walk down the narrow aisle. Seat 3B. When I take my seat, I also take the champagne for departure and drink it quicker than is socially acceptable in this part of the plane.

I did what I could. I went where I needed to go, and I even tried to put this venture behind me and live my life like an ordinary thirty-year-old. But turns out an ordinary life, with a house and husband and a nine to five wasn't for me. Visions of my parents battling to keep their house and business afloat protrude through my closed eyelids. Memories of poor years in trade, Mum cheating and finding a life of her own. People suck. Life sucks. And I've been spending more than half of mine trying to be one step ahead of death. And I don't even have a life to show for it.

The flight attendant closes the door when all the passengers are on board, and I catch the attention of the man serving in first class. I order a double vodka tonic and a blanket so I can wrap myself up and drown my sorrows. I wasted the life I had. There were so many times I wanted to go back and revisit places, been braver and explored more. But I didn't. I kept my promise to Liam and never went backwards. Except for now. This is one huge backwards step. I visited just about every square foot on land along the equator line, and sailed through Null Island and the surrounding water of the 0/0 location, but there was nothing that gave me any sort of resonating feeling that Liam talked about. No place that felt like I was being pulled in or anchored to the earth. No solid place I wanted to stay, if that felt like home. Well, except for Sao Tome Principe.

My vodka tonic is placed in front of me, on top of a thick napkin, and I stare at the plushness of such an everyday item. The smell of lavender hits me and I think I'm imagining it. I pick up my drink to sniff, hoping that the smell of vodka will overpower, but the flight attendant lets me know its lavender flavoured tonic. I close my eyes and sigh, like I'm about to move from one yoga pose to another, and inhale through my nose, taking a sip. The bitterness gets stuck in the back of my throat and I can't even enjoy one thing that used to mean so much to me. I'm being told about the new product line from a company I don't want to hear anything about, so I just hand the drink back to the attendant. 'Just plain tonic, if you have it, please. Otherwise cola will do.'

I've never managed to communicate with Liam as easily as I hoped. I tried to make mistakes, to get more tapes and information from Liam. I've tried putting myself in danger—well controlled danger, like bungee jumping and skydiving, but nothing left me with another sonnet from the man I've always dreamed of meeting.

The tapes showed up in my past in the most mundane times, and the more I thought about it, maybe those un-extraordinary days are the days that most of us die. The times when nothing special happens. The time when we are least expecting it, as we're doing the simplest things, like crossing the road or walking down the stairs too fast. Perhaps I got those warnings exactly when I needed them. I hope I'm right. Because going home to Mike is a pretty mundane task after travelling the world. And if it's truly a mistake, Liam will tell me, right?

The roar of the engine vibrates through the cabin, as the plane begins its taxi around the runway. The flight crew are doing last-minute stowing of items and everyone else is settled, ready to go. Apart from me. I don't want to go, but I don't want to stay either.

I thought of when I decided to go home, and no new tapes showed up in my bag. I took it a step further and told Mike and Audrey and the kids on a Skype call that I was coming back to L.A. Even in the middle of the call, I found my attention drifting towards my bag to see if anything had shown up.

Booking the tickets and riding to the airport. Going through security and sitting at the gate. All the time checking for a sign I need to not give up and go home. The itch under my skin pulls at my anxiety to check my bag and Walkman one last time. To make sure that this is the decision I'm supposed to make. But there is nothing new there. Just like always.

There's grief in my heart that I can't speak to Liam. That I can't communicate with him like I thought I could. That he has power over me and I've never even met him. The flight attendant mistakes my emotions for panic and tries to reassure me before take-off. I simply nod and let her think whatever she wants. Nothing even gets close to explaining a lifetime of chasing someone else's woes.

I'm defeated and I can feel the symptoms of depression seeking into my core. At first, I thought I was just feeling sorry for myself and lonely. But when the feelings stick with you for years, you've got to realise what it is. No point in thinking it's a bad spell. I need help, and I'm not getting it on my own.

I don't know what I'm more disappointed about. That nothing Liam has warned me about has come to pass, or that I was stupid enough to believe in this otherworldly life.

Of course, nothing time travelley or alternative reality has come from my research. I've not bumped into an American trying to save my life. I've not died or had a near death experience. I've not had anything remotely traumatic happen to me these last seven years of traipsing around the equator trying to find answers to a riddle from a childhood fantasy.

I've been had. It's like one big con that was my life, but I still don't know what the payoff was for the guy on the tapes.

I never went back to the same place twice. I did my research thoroughly and methodically each time I went somewhere new. I thought and planned out each trip and day, so that I would miss nothing and feel the need to double-check.

I also never went backwards in my thoughts. I never dwelled on things, and I kept myself and my research moving forward at all times. It didn't make a bit of difference. I'm still the same, and I'm still not any closer to anything.

The only thing I ever second-guessed was Liam himself. Why did he do this to me? Why did I put my whole life on hold and fall madly in love with someone who wasn't even real?

Mike's house is everything you expect from a movie millionaire, and I have my own room with living space and bathroom.

The kids video called me last week to let me know they were decorating it for me coming home. I was excited to come back to them. To feel like I have some family who will be happy to see me.

The Uber ride from the airport to Beverly Hills doesn't take as long as I remember from before, and the driver gets us through the bottom gates and driving up Mike's driveway. When I open his front door, I breathe in the cool air conditioning.

'Hello, bitches, I'm home,' I call out.

'Caitlyn?' I hear Mike calling through the house and he appears in the reception area within a few seconds. Mike ages every time I see him, but I guess leaving years between visits will do that to you. Each time I see him, in real life or on screen, he looks different. Always changing for a role. He grabs hold of me and swings me around the air. Hugging me tight, I sink into him for much-needed comfort, but he grabs the back of my head and messes up my hair. Typical.

'Back in one piece, I see. I can't believe you've been backpacking for so long. Who knew one continent could keep a really annoying person so busy?'

David and Stella join us in the hallway, and I glance at them to say hello and answer my brother. Now there is a power couple for you. David always was attractive, and he's got better with age. He and Stella are made for each other. Or were. The power couple who made groundbreaking careers are as beautiful on the outside as they are inside. Who dressed for success and negotiated the deals they wanted and still managed to make it home for 5:00 p.m. to co-parent their kid, Max. Even though David was only married to Stella for a year, and Max is his stepson.

'Well, I had to come pay you back eventually.' He'll never take it back.

'Hmm, I was wondering if that was ever going to come up.' He smirks and I punch him in the arm. My fingers crack under the contact and I curse. David has to be the best-looking guy on TV. Not that I like him, he's always been Mike's friend rather than anything else, but I love how the two of them haven't changed a bit with the fame and money and the pull that L.A. can have on some people.

'Jeez, Mike,' David says. 'Her bags are barely even in the door. Give her five minutes before you launch into the sensible brother routine.'

'No,' I bellow. 'I need a job, and since I owe you a ton of money, I was thinking you'd be more inclined to give me my old job back.' I clasp my hands in mock pleading and plaster a fake smile on my face, knowing that it doesn't reach my eyes, let alone into the core of my body.

'You want me to pay you, so you can pay me back? How the hell does that work?'

76

I take Mike's arm and catch Stella's in the other, walking the two of them towards the kitchen.

'Can you grab those?' I ask David about my bags. 'There's more outside.'

'What were you guys all doing home in the middle of the day?' I sink into the couch of the window seats and curl up. Despite being on a flight forever, I still need to make myself small and tight, so I don't feel like I'm falling apart. 'I was expecting Audrey and the kids.'

'Audrey is at the charity office,' Mike says. 'And the kids are in school. Well, the girls are in school. Andrew's in day care one day a week when Audrey has to go in to the office. Mostly I work from home when I'm not on set.'

'Oh good, that's kind of convenient if I move into the guest house.'

'Caitlyn, you can't just come back and work for me. You were gone for years. I had to replace you.'

I pause the twirl of my new purple hair extensions and place my hand on my heart. 'You can't replace your own sister, Michael.'

'Ha-ha,' Mike mocks.

'I'll have a look at things and see if I have some jobs for you,' Stella butts in. 'And David too. I'm sure between the three of us, we can pull a full-time job together.'

'Thank you, thank you.' I try to get excited and bounce in my seat, knowing that these three won't let something like a twenty-year jet lag impede a day's work.

'Okay, but you can start with David. He doesn't have a P.A. and I'm sure once you start doing all his shit for him, he'll realise he needs one. Then he's the one stuck paying you,' Mike says.

'Great! He always did love me.'

'Come on. I'll help you make up the bed in the guest house, and you can tell me all about the asshole.'

'What asshole?'

Stella pulls me up off the seat and facing her. 'The one who had you pack up and come home all of a sudden.'

I shake my head. Guess I'm not hiding my low mood as well as I thought. Outside the kitchen, in the garden leading to the pool house, I pause and take a deep breath. 'God, I love this house.' The weather and scenery of California's nice. Not as peaceful as I've been used to, but the strong sun and cool breeze make it one nice place to spend some years.

David finally returns from the hallway. 'You didn't tell me you had a cab full of bags, Perra, and no cab fare,' he calls after us.

I blow him a kiss through the patio doors and laugh. 'Thanks, boss,' I call out. 'I'll make sure and earn it back.'

David looks dumbfounded, and Stella and I chuckle as we walk over to the pool house, leaving Mike to explain to David about his new hire.

Despite knowing David since Mike was in college, most of my time in L.A. I spent avoiding him and Stella. Since Liam told me when I was a teenager that Mike would marry a woman called Audrey, and David a woman called Stella, all before his untimely time-travel related death, the supernatural tingles would run through me anytime I saw them together. David never stops working, so it was easy to avoid him when I lived in L.A. before, but now I'll be working directly for him.

Stella helps me unpack and I avoid any conversation about men who might have broken my heart and stick with the scripted reason for my sudden return. *I got fed up and wanted to come home and be a grownup for once.* Pretty easy to accept since they don't know what I've really being doing for so long. Or how well I did it.

Three hours after I landed and I'm put to work. David wants me to deliver documents over to his lab at UCLA, but typically he doesn't have any time to train me. I saw it so many times when I was a P.A. We got to know each other, the assistants to the celebrities. You could always tell if it was their first time on the job. They would scramble around trying to figure out what to do and who to call, and in this instance, where your boss's office is. The only way to survive was to make friends with other P.A.s, and that became your most valuable asset. If people liked *you*, you got the things your boss wanted quicker.

I was always lucky, though.

David apparently takes security seriously, and Stella wants to introduce me personally to David's team, so they know what information and documents I can have access to, and what things I can courier across the city if needed. I'm waiting for a security door to open from the other end while Stella is rattling off instructions for me.

Holy hell, that is one hot piece of science guy. Looking every bit of the one-night stand I used to drool over, the guy opening the door is hipster and cool, wrapped up in a muscular burrito. 'Well, hello. Wouldn't mind doing him some damage.'

Top knot hair and a short beard hide the most beautiful face that could be attached to someone.

'That's Liam,' Stella says and my insides freeze. Stella keeps talking as I try to breathe. My heart is beating hard against my chest. I wonder if Stella can hear it. I try not to melt into a puddle of everlasting hope and desire like I did the first three times I met a hottie called Liam. It's been a while since I've crossed paths with a William or Liam. Especially an American. The first Liam I met was before I even left Blackpool and was still an adorably annoying teenager. But he was English and old and friends with my dad. When he opened his mouth to speak, I sulked away in a huff.

The second one, and third actually, was only last year, when I had an impromptu trip to London. An author, Carl Wilson was writing a book about time travel theories and had seen some of my YouTube videos on my travels around the equator. I mentioned a few things in them he thought might be cool for his next novel and flew me out to meet him. It was a nice break after watching my dreams and life burn to the ground.

Stella's still talking to me as I'm staring at the hottie.

'He's David's lab assistant. Well, to be honest, he's like another David. He knows everything around here, and he's the only person David has ever relinquished control to.'

I try to play it cool for Stella. 'Urgh, I'd so relinquish control to him, too.'

'Caitlyn. Seriously, can you cut the crap?'

'Sorry.' I smile and take a calming breath. It has to be him, right? The scientist who happens to know my brother and his friends, who is working with David on time travel theories? I'll know. As soon as he speaks, I'll know his voice.

The guy leaves the inner office and greets us at the security door. 'Hi, Stella.'

'Liam, this is David's new personal assistant.'

He holds out his hand, grinning, and my ovaries pop. The butterflies deep inside my belly churn lower. I never expected him to be so attractive. I knew I would have had a connection to him, but I never expected it to be a real insta-attraction thing too. Maybe the jet lag and tiredness are making me see things that might not be there as he's hardly spoken, but I swear it *could* be him. Real-Liam or not, I really want to get to know this guy, be damned if it will mess with my head.

'Nice to meet you.' His gaze drops to our hands, and he takes his time, scrolling back up to my face.

'Can you make sure she has access here? David sent her over with files for you. I'm only here to show her around today. She'll be doing most of the drops from now on. David's going to be busy at home for the next few months and he needs someone to run back and forth.'

Liam's eyes widen and he looks at Stella. 'You're telling me I can send everything I need through Caitlyn, instead of waiting for you or Mike or god forbid having to drive over there myself?'

Oh my, the way he said my name. I need to hear him say it again.

'Exactly,' I tell him. 'Use me for whatever you need.' I'm blushing, I'm sure, but I mean it. Liam puts his hands in his pockets and rocks back on his heels, smiling at me.

'So.' Stella clears her throat. 'I have a lot to do. If you two want to get this over with, we can go.'

'Get what over with?' I ask.

She nods to Liam. 'Ask her out.'

'Stella.' I gasp, spinning to face her.

'I know you want him to ask you out. And you.' Stella turns to Liam. 'This is the quietest two minutes I've ever heard you, so I know you want to ask her.'

I hide my smile behind my hand. 'I would say yes. Just so you know.'

Liam blows out a gasp. 'Good.'

'Good,' Stella repeats. 'So, if you can get the access sorted and send it over to Mike's house. Better still, drop it off yourself tonight when you're done, and you can pick her up for your date. Now, if I've finished matchmaking, I have a job to do.'

'You're Mike's assistant too?' Liam asks.

I snort. 'Not anymore. I quit on him a few years ago. It was a last-minute thing, and I left him hanging. He won't re-hire me, so David's stuck with me.'

Liam tilts his head. 'You quit, but he lets you hang around his house, and David trusts you with trailing his life's work from one end of the city to another. What'd you do? Cast a spell on them?'

'She's Mike's sister,' Stella tells him.

'Caitlyn Knight?' he asks, his voice a little hoarse. Understanding lights up his face. 'Of course you are.'

'Don't worry,' Stella says. 'Mike won't be mad you asked his sister out.' She pauses. 'Will he?' she asks me.

I shrug. 'I don't know. Boys usually go missing after they ask me out. I never get the chance to find out what Mike thinks.'

We both giggle, but Liam's turned ashen.

'Don't be such a scaredy cat. She's joking,' Stella says.

'I'll see you tonight.' He grins at me.

We turn to the main door and head outside.

'Wear something warm,' he calls after us. 'I'm going to take you somewhere a little unexpected.'

'God, that smile is lethal.' I pant to Stella once we are out of earshot. 'I wonder how many different ways I can get him to smile like that.'

Stella laughs. 'You've turned into a piranha.'

Actually, I was a fully committed, fully loved up fool until a guy brought out my worst fears about myself. But if she wants to think I've been carefree forever, then at least she won't ask any deep questions. I nudge her in the side. 'Only when they ask nicely.'

CHAPTER
NINE

The rest of the day, thoughts of Liam being real-Liam make my head spin and I am a little unsteady on my feet. I wonder if it is entirely possible that the part of my life where Liam said we might one day meet and become friends has actually come about. Although he always said I was dead before it happened in his alternate life. Even if the person I met today was, in fact, Liam, it's a different version of himself. One that has no idea who I am. How important those tapes were to make. How important he was to me.

I try to get through day one of my new job without screwing anything up. Lucky for me, David lives on the same street as Mike, so my commute to work is five minutes. Exactly what I'm used to, although it's particularly noteworthy in L.A. I can totally handle that. The most productive thing I've done so far is to create an email address and write a list of all the things I want to buy for the office. Stationery shopping is fun and wasn't necessary when I was setting up the farm in Sao Tome and Principe.

My mind wanders back there at least once a day since I left. There are so many memories that anything can trigger my longing for the place. It was the one time I felt like I had found a place to call home, only it turned out it was someone else's home and I was the piece on the side. Six years, I was the mistress and I had no idea. Six years he was stealing our business's money, and I had no clue. Every memory of the place I loved gets me infuriated now. I was on a mission to learn about instincts and supernatural pulls. And I had the wool pulled over me.

I tap on the computer and finish some office shopping as a distraction. I ordered a mug for my coffee that says *I'm the real boss*. David's not bad. He'll find it funny. He'll probably steal it and sharpie his name all over it so I won't want to use it anymore.

Science documentaries are not exactly a hot commodity in the mainstream, but David made it work. It is of course because he is gorgeous and rich and owns a TV network, but he has brought science into the pop culture, and for that, he deserves the TV awards. I can't help but think the real brains behind David's and Mike's careers is Stella. She's the only manager who ever took either of them seriously, and look at what careers she's built with them! Maybe I'll ask her for some career advice. You know, after I've settled into the job they all gave me, no questions asked. Or maybe she knows a lawyer who can get me my company back.

I'm trying to find something to do in the outer office, to make it look like I'm working, but I'm still really unsure about what my job is or what David wants me to do. Liam and his dad, Ethan, and Stella showed up ten minutes ago and are all with him in the office, so I really don't want to look like a slacker in front of them. I tidy out the desk drawer and organise some Post-it notes. The outer office looks like supplies only, and nothing I can mess up by rearranging, so I get to it.

Sitting in a high back rolling office chair, I realise that my career choice has been all wrong. Focusing on good mental health stimulants was great until I could no longer stand the smell of my own products with the memories it invoked.

Maybe a TV scientist is the way to go. I bet this chair cost more than my bed. It glides across the floor to the other side of the room without a hitch. I dip my head to the lower drawer and pull out a stack of printer paper and hear the others talking in the office.

'We need to find out where and make sure Caitlyn goes with them.'

Liam's voice from inside the office, where I'm not distracted by his face, is so bloody obvious that I stop breathing. I slide off the chair silently and take a step towards the door, leaning in so I can hear more. I hear the voice I've listened to over and over for years. When I lean on the door and know that Liam is on the other side, my Liam, the real-Liam, with the real-Liam voice, my insides calm and I know I'm exactly where I'm supposed to be.

'Make sure she's safe because right now, she's the one I'm worried about the most,' Liam says.

'You don't have to do this, David,' Stella speaks. 'It's too dangerous.' They talk back and forth, something about Audrey and the butterfly effect and I strain to make out the full conversation word for word, but I hear Liam say he saw me disappear when he time travelled as a boy.

I feel like I should sit down before I fall over, but I can't miss anything they are saying. I realise I'm not breathing, which is a stupid response to finding out that everything is real, and the people I was worried about already know what's going on. I inhale deeply and let my breath out slowly. I strain to hear the rest of what they're saying. David and Stella might just be in trouble like Liam always said, and finally, I'm in the place I should be to help.

'*Not* changing one small thing can change everything as well.' David speaks about...living a future, and Stella's and Max's lives. The universe and realities and alternative futures. It's everything I've been trying to find out most of my life and ran halfway around the world to find and apparently the people in my life already knew as well.

They're moving around the room, still talking about David's research that he's not shown them before, time travelling and Audrey and something about a crash.

David pushes the door open and catches me listening in to their conversation. I'm not even sorry.

'I was there?' I ask Liam. He knows me. This version of Liam knows me too. Or some part of me. 'It took me a long time to find you. All I ever knew was your first name.'

'What do you mean, find me?' Liam steps towards me.

My heart sinks into the depth of my stomach, and the thud makes me want to puke.

Time travel and alternative realities.

This isn't the same version of Liam who was talking to me. His Caitlyn was dead, and he never met me.

There's a version of me out there that never got the warnings and is already dead. He saved the wrong Caitlyn. And I've seen her die in my dreams.

'You left me a bunch of tapes when I was a kid. You said I was going to save David's life one day. And that I needed to be ready. I needed to figure out how to anchor myself to him or we'd both get lost forever in the switch.'

'The switch?' Stella asks.

'Between realities,' I tell her. 'Versions of the future. That our families would shift between a few of them, and I had to make sure I went along too.'

'What tapes are you talking about?' Liam asks.

'Information on where to go, what to look for. How to harness the ability to control movements in time.'

'To travel by proxy?' Liam's eyes narrow. 'And you're coming too?'

86

'You said in the tapes that Mike never travelled with you in the crash, and it was lucky he didn't or there would have been a conflict.'

'What conflict?' Stella says.

'That he was in love with someone called Audrey, and that he'd be focused on trying to find and save her. His energy would pull us apart. But I travelled there with you, and once we found ourselves at a dinner party, I had to know what to do to bring David home.'

'That's where you've been these years?' David asks. 'Travelling for Liam's research?'

I nod. 'I never knew that you all understood what was going on, or I would have come to you for help. I thought I was on my own.' I kick my feet around. 'Honestly, I never really knew if it was true or if I was chasing someone else's crazy dream. Until Mike married Audrey, and then I knew I had to keep going.'

'Huh. This is interesting,' Stella says.

'What is?' Liam's Dad, Ethan, asks.

'Them two. They were the only ones together in both versions of a future that David visited.' Stella smiles tightly. 'It's like, out of everyone, they are the ones who were really meant to be together.'

I shake my head. 'We're not together. We've never met properly.'

'No, but the moment you did, the two of you were interested in each other.' Stella folds her arms. 'And you were the only ones in the other future that could have had a relationship without the interference of time travel. It's just, I don't know. A little disappointing that the rest of us don't get that guarantee too.'

There's no guarantee in life. Not even when you think you have it all planned out.

Liam and his dad go to David's upstairs office. The one in the attic I was told not to go into. Guess I know why. On the way, Liam calls for me to get my coat. Butterflies whirl in my stomach. How the hell can he be thinking of a date after what I just admitted to him? I sounded like a psychopath. I take a deep breath and slip off my flip-flops that I've been using as slippers around the house. If I need a coat, something warm, then I'm going to have to go with sensible shoes, too.

I'm ready to go, and it's after 5:00 p.m. when Liam and Ethan come down the stairs. There is a deathly silence between them, and Ethan leaves without saying goodbye.

I'm too busy checking out his son to really be bothered about it. Liam is not just the hot guy I imagined him to be, he is a legit drop-the-panties gorgeous man. There is a smooth movement with his strides, that hint to a well-kept body under that dress shirt. Paired with worn jeans and loose boots, it completes the hipster look. Man bun, tattooed arms, and enough stubble to burn the thighs and I'm clenching in my seat. But that damn smile flips my stomach. Butterflies are so pre-teen. Stomach flipping, clit throbbing smiles are what I'm into these days.

'You don't have a car available, do you?' he asks. 'Turns out I didn't plan this well, and my dad's stormed off with the car I drove here.'

Despite living in America for a while before my travels, the accent still gets me. It's been so long since I've been surrounded by this familiarity that I drown in the sweetness of his voice.

I smile back at him and stand up. 'Sure do.' I show him the car keys Mike gave me earlier.

He holds his arm out, letting me move past him and ushering me to the door. 'I'll show you the way.'

Liam gives me directions, and we're driving back to UCLA. Early evening means there is still loads of traffic on the roads, and it's hot out. I'm not used to driving so far. The islet off Sao Tome and Principe where I spent so much time growing my life and business was only two miles long. Even when we used the Jeeps, it was only for a short drive or to move produce.

The number of cars and trucks on the highway gives me a little driving anxiety. It's been so long since I wasn't the only person on the road. Talking of people. They are everywhere. Standing on the sidewalk, waiting to cross at junctions. Outside shops, carpooling, and crammed on buses that we pass.

I forget just how many people must be on the planet, but it feels like they are all here.

Sitting with Liam is comfortable. I'm not a huge talker anymore, and I like that we can drive and let our minds wander. The noise of traffic outside and the chatter of a gang of students we pass at the lights has me closing the window for some quiet time. I switch on the air con for a breeze, but I don't think we need much. L.A. isn't that hot in September. Well, not as hot as the tropical climate I'm used to. The air con in Mike's car is strong and I have to lower it down to stop myself from freezing in the car. I wonder if Liam is too hot. I glance over at him, but he doesn't look uncomfortable. Just contemplating. He has that stern, concentrated look on his face, and it's pretty sexy to know how much information might be in that brain.

'What did I tell you? On the tapes you said I left?' Liam asks.

'You haven't recorded them yet,' I tell him. 'Or it might not even be this version of you that does. You explained all about alternative dimensions and realities. I think maybe something went wrong. And it was a different version of you that reached out to me.' I shrug, trying to play off the devastation that the last twenty years of my life were wasted.

'If you let me listen to the tapes and all the things you wish I told you, I can maybe fill in the blanks if I have the answers. Maybe if the time comes for me to record them, I won't miss anything you need.'

I shrug. 'You said that information can only come at the right time. And honestly, I kind of get that now.' I twist to the side, looking at Liam, and back at the road.

'Maybe now is the right time. Maybe there are things on there that David and I haven't found out yet. That will help further our research before the end of the year.'

I nod to him and tilt my head to my bag on the passenger floor. My old Walkman is in there with the three tapes I have from Liam and fresh batteries. I knew he would want to hear them. It doesn't take him long to adjust the headset and settle in to listen while I drive.

I can tell what he's listening to. I know it practically by heart. How he explains his work with his father. And his research on harnessing the earth's core. How their theory on different cross sections of the earth might hold different energy. To look at the equator line in particular, over the meridian lines, which are technically anywhere. How they looked into the magnetic energy of the poles and need to rely on expert excursions out there, least of all that I wouldn't survive long if I tried to trek out there. He explained how to measure and record energy levels on a spectroscopy, and the importance of high energy atmospheric readings. I see him skip through the music breaks he gave me all those years ago, and when he reaches the last tape, he looks crestfallen. We only have time to listen to one of the sides of the tape and when it clicks off, Liam doesn't turn it over yet.

'All of this is so basic, we covered it all years ago. I don't even understand what I needed you to find for us,' he says.

My stomach sinks and I feel defensive over the Liam who recorded this for me. The Liam and the tapes that I lived my life by for so long.

'Whatever I went to find out, I probably wouldn't have looked so long or hard had I known where and when to find you. I might have found you first and not learned anything different. I know it doesn't feel like it, but I need to have faith that something I did or learned is going to come in useful, or like you said, already saved my life.'

He nods. 'I just hope that if it was a different version of me, I figure out that I need to record the tapes in the first place.'

'You already did. So don't worry.'

He rubs his head. 'You know, time travel loops and implications and the grandfather theory have all been weighing on my mind since I was ten. You would think I would have it figured out by now. But most of it has been theory. Now that I'm trying to implement things, the worry and anxiety are back.'

'Worry about what?' I turn to look at him.

'What if I got it all wrong?'

'I know the feeling.'

Driving towards campus, I slow down and we pass a strip of takeout restaurants. The overwhelming scent of the combined foods wafts through the car and I'm suddenly craving some good old-fashioned junk food.

I park outside the planetarium. It's still warm, but the sun will set soon, and I'm glad I opted for thick tights under my denim shorts. My leather jacket is short and bunches at my waist, but it will keep me warm enough. We look like a couple already. You know when you stand next to someone and you just fit? Like everything about your personalities just matches.

'Is it weird that I feel like I know you so well?'

Liam grins. 'Not really. I mean, I need to know more about what you know about me, but I kind of have the same feeling.'

I snort. Teenage obsession is hard to beat.

'This place is beautiful.' I look up at the white dome on top of the otherwise regular building in awe. I smile tentatively at him. 'I mean the potential of what you can see. The beauty in the universe that's hidden from most of us. When I come across a lookout, I'm always taken aback by the idea of what's waiting for me.'

Liam takes my hand and strokes his thumb over the back of my fingers. Shivers run over my body and instead of throwing myself into his arms, like I've been waiting to do my whole life, Stella's words ring alarm bells at the back of my head. *Meant to be together*. I pull my hand back slowly so as not to give off any malice in the retreat. But I don't want to be with someone out of fate. I want to fall in love and be swept off my feet.

I'm not a sure thing.

'Sorry,' Liam says, and I start to tell him it's okay, but I stop myself. I don't need to apologise.

'There's a show starting in twenty minutes.' He nods to the door. 'Let's eat out here on the bench. I want to go get the keys first, before everyone else gets here, too.'

I nod and let Liam lead the way. The butterflies well and truly landed with a disappointing thud in my core.

'Keys for what?'

'The roof,' he says. 'I like to go up there and think about things after the presentations. Being outside in the air—'

'Helps clear the thoughts. Connect you to the universe. I know. I was on my own a lot, so I got to really digest the information I was finding. Only I'm more of a grounding sort of person. Standing on the ground, the dirt or grass. My friend Natalie taught me to kick off my shoes and connect my feet with the earth. I guess you're more of a space guy?' I nod to the sky above, showing the vast outer space that's above and all around us.

Liam bites the side of his lip like he was going to say something and is literally chewing it over.

'I just dropped a bomb on you guys that I know all about time travel and what you've been studying for years. And that you've been a part of my life in that regard. You can ask me awkward questions if you need to.'

Liam holds the glass door open as we cross inside and he moves towards a staff door at the back of the hallway. 'I know. I just want this to be a proper date, too.'

I've realised what it is about Liam's smile that's so lethal. It's that he's already a good-looking guy, but the smile pinches his cheeks into dimples, and you can see all the way to the depths of his soul. His face becomes more personality than looks, and man, that guy is hot all the way to the gooey centre. The butterflies stir again, and I tap them down. 'Let's make sure we get along then, before any of this *meant to be* crap gets in the way.'

Liam pulls open a key box inside what looks to be a janitor's closet and pockets a bunch of keys while he answers. 'Of course. Wouldn't want the universe to screw anything up, right?'

'Like me dying?' I quip with a drawn-out slowness.

Liam stops beside me. 'What?'

'You know, the whole, *do as I tell you because you're going to die* thing.'

93

Liam takes my elbow and pulls me around to face him fully. 'Who told you that?' There's urgency in his voice. Like he thinks I've been threatened, and he's going to swoop in and save the day.

He must forget that I'm a Knight, and we save ourselves.

I bounce from one foot to the next. Trying to think how I can word this, without ruining our dating life before we've even gone into the venue. 'You did,' I speak softly but confidently. I'm not scared anymore. I don't really know what I feel about the last twenty years of my life.

'It was the entire premise of the tapes you left me when I was a teenager. You said that I was dead in your reality and you never met me. That things were wrong, and I had to figure out how to switch realities back where they were supposed to be.'

Liam's face has fallen, and I can see that hurt and disappointment all the way to his soul.

'Although you never said how I died. Or where. Or when. So basically I've been living with death hanging over me all this time, and honestly, I've been through all the emotions. And thoughts about this being a cruel prank or a warning from an angel. But now, I'm just tired. I have a whole host of information about the earth's equator and natural phenomena and occurrences and beauties of the worlds. I know all about sinkholes and optical illusions of water over craters in the ocean floor. I know the physics of how the northern lights work and why we can only see so much of the light spectrum. I know enough about South America I could open my own tour company. I even sat down to theorise a book with a tech CEO in England on working manmade time travel electronics to open up natural wormholes. That was actually a fun year. I got to spend a lot of time with another person on that project.' My smile is ironic.

'Things are crossing over way more than I ever thought. I was sure there was such an obvious line between the alternative future I visited when I was a kid. But now we know that soon David will start travelling into the past, and this. It adds a layer of complexity that we've never foreseen.'

'I just want to get back to what my life could have been if I never wasted twenty years chasing something that might not even exist.'

'But here you are, one day back in your normal life, and you find me.'

I nod. 'That's the scary part. Because I thought if it was still a lie and waste of my life, then we were okay.'

'You are okay.' Liam steps forward. 'I said that you died before I met you. And now we've met, which must mean you saved your life.' He smiles. 'It worked.'

'Maybe.' I swallow. 'But there were so many other things I had to do, people to save. And I have this feeling that it's not even started yet.'

Liam nods and tugs me inside the janitor's closet, closing the door behind us. 'I think you're right.'

There is contentment with being shut in a quiet room with Liam, no outside distractions or sounds to interrupt us.

'I saw you when I was a kid. And nothing about this time travel line, or realities, has been simple. Stella has met a future version of David throughout her life, and our David here has never time travelled before. Audrey has popped up in Mike's past so many times, but she too has no idea about time travel. There seem to be incidents for all of us. Now seems like the time it might be starting for *us*.'

'I'm safe here, in this reality. But not our friends.'

95

'I think that's where you were getting dragged to when I saw you in the other reality. You were going to fix it all.'

'And get David,' I tell him.

'Why? What's wrong with David?'

'He was murdered. In the past.' Liam flinches. 'Dad and I remember, but David gave us strict instructions not to tell him or Stella when our timeline catches up.' He shuffles forward and takes my hand. 'You can't tell anyone, Caitlyn. You have to promise.'

'How can I not tell David he's going to die?' I pull back. 'Why tell me in the past if it's not to change things?'

Liam shakes his head. 'Dad and I have known for years, so there must be another reason I told you.'

I swallow thickly and look up, trying to avoid eye contact.

'What?' he says. 'What do you know?'

'You told me I need to steal his body.'

CHAPTER

TEN

The planetarium show on the centre of the galaxy wasn't enough of a distraction, and I could tell that Liam, too, was only half listening. We've been on the roof for ten minutes afterward. Liam, sitting on the plastic chair, looking up at the sky, thinking, is calming.

I stare at him and know that with any other guy on any other date, this would be the point we kiss. We're staring at each other, but instead of thinking about how I want to devour him and taste him, I'm thinking about if I want to marry him. Of course, there is a part of me that's always wanted him. But now that it's here in front of me, I'm not even sure I'm ready to settle down with my soulmate, or whatever he might be.

I laugh out loud at the ridiculousness of it, and Liam's eyebrows furrow.

'What's so funny?' he asks.

'Nothing.' My laugher dies down to chuckles. Take it slow. One date at a time. 'I've just had fun tonight, despite everything. It's been a long time since I just had this comfortable silence. Usually I need to keep going, keep moving, just to keep my head silent. This is much safer than my usual pastimes.'

Liam's eyebrows dart up. 'What are your usual pastimes?'

'Anything physical that will leave me exhausted.'

Liam tilts his head and holds back what he was about to say.

'Adventure stuff. Hiking and running. But when I first moved to South America, I was involved with a tour company. We added on longer tours and adventure sports. Skydiving and bungee jumping. And volcano surfing. That one was a real money spinner.'

'What the hell is volcano surfing?' Liam leans forward.

'Inactive volcanoes, obviously,' I tell him. 'The outer side of some of the volcano mountains is covered in ash. It's like black sand. We got a few buggies, drove people up to the top, and let them surf down the volcano on a board. But there were a lot of treks and trips around the Ecuador volcanoes that were purely for scenic purposes. We even had a ten-day tour that followed the equator line all the way through the Amazon. I got paid to do the things I wanted to do.'

'How very entrepreneurial of you.'

I laugh. 'Well, I prefer to be called adventurous. Or fearless. I'll need to find some places I can hike around here. I'll be needing more time out in the open. One day back, and I can feel pressured in by all the buildings and people.'

'I can bring you a few places I know.'

'Great. It's my birthday next week. You can bring me on another date.' I smile over at him.

'Absolutely.' He smiles back. 'What day is your birthday?'

'Wednesday,' I tell him.

'The twenty-third? Your birthday is on September twenty-third? That's crazy. We're half-birthday twins.' He laughs.

'What the hell is a half-birthday twin?'

'I was born on March twenty-third, on the summer equinox. It's the longest day of the year, well, one of the two longest days. Yours is the other one. How old are you turning?'

'Thirty-six,' I say.

Liam nods. 'Nineteen-eighty really turned out to be some year for us. Equinox babies born on the same day as the earth's rotation equals the sun in the same proportions. That's crazy. And it makes you a Libra?' he asks.

'I guess. I never really paid attention to the star signs.'

'What?' Liam practically yells. 'How can you not pay attention to the star signs? It's literally the alignment of the sky and the earth. Day and night and the earth rotation. Don't you think that our position on earth on specific times has any meaning?'

'I suppose. I mean, I'll need to look into it now that you're so convinced that it's special.'

I pull out my phone and start searching for Libra's characteristics. 'What star sign are you?' I ask.

'Aries,' he tells me. 'And the equinox is Mars.' He chuckles. And yours is Venus, which is fitting.'

My eyes dart off the screen and I place my phone down on the plastic chair.

'What?' Liam asks.

'Nothing, it's just stupid horoscope things. You never mentioned it having any relevance before, so it must just be consumer crap.'

Liam takes my phone before I've realised and he looks at the page I was reading about Aries men and Libra women being highly sexually compatible with instant attraction, and I see the moment he reads that and puts the phone back down.

'Do you know what I'm really worried about?' Liam's voice is full of promised confessions.

'What?' I ask.

99

'I don't want to make a mistake. If everything has happened in the past and in the loops for a reason, then when I saw you in trouble in some alternative future, I'm scared I might not be able to stop it from happening.'

'Because it already happened.' I sit up and lean forward. 'Maybe that's when I leave to help David. Maybe that's what I need to wait for?'

Liam nods. 'I guess we need to get you ready so you know what you're doing.'

'Anchor me,' I tell him. 'You told me in the tapes I had to figure out what and who my anchor was, so I don't get lost.'

'Why do you think I was the one who recorded the tapes for you?' he asks.

'I'm not sure.' I shrug. 'I only met you today. It's not like we have some bond or anything.'

'I met you years ago. Saw you at least. When I was a kid, I travelled into the future and I saw you. I thought you were so cool. I wanted to be someone who could get your attention. You were with a guy, and I was so annoyed at him for being with you, but not helping you when time slowed down and you seemed to get pulled away from your friends.'

I hold my breath as he tells me something solid about my future. Something that I've never had before.

'As I grew up, I tried to dress like him and be like him, until one day I realised I was him. It was me who was with you in the future. You and I, right now, look exactly like we did that day in the future that I saw.'

'And we were together, like Stella said we were? Married?'

Liam smiles. 'Not married. We were meeting for the first time. But I liked you. The boy who was snooping on your conversation and the man that I was sitting next to you. And the man I am right here with you now.'

100

I swallow hard. I want to let him know I like him, too. That it's been one day, and years, for me.

Liam stands up and takes my hand. Pulling me up and into his space, he looks down at my face.

The heat that bursts through my chest at the closeness to him is incontrollable and I lunge to his mouth. I attack his lips and he opens for me, sliding his tongue inside my mouth. He tastes like fresh air and heat. Like the elements of the earth that I've chased around the world. I moan and run my fingers into his hair, tugging his head closer to mine so that there isn't an inch of space for us to separate. Our entire bodies are pressed together and I can feel him grow hard against my stomach. I rise onto my tiptoes, pushing my body higher so I can rub against him, and he helps me. A hand under my ass, and he's hitched me off the ground, pressing my core against his and pulling his head back for air. We don't move away from each other. He holds me tight and looks from my eyes to my mouth and back again.

Drops of rain fall from the sky, and I pull back. The rain falls fast and heavy on top of us, and Liam keeps me in his arms. He's not taken his eyes off me and he leans back in for another kiss. Heavy and fast, the rain pours down on us and we're getting soaked.

'We're not getting married,' I tell him.

He smiles and nods. 'Okay.'

Grinning. 'This is going to be one step at a time.'

'I can do that.' He swipes the water off my face.

'Well, I mean maybe a few steps at a time. I'm not saying I want this to be slow. It's the whole future things that freak me out—'

Liam cuts me off with another kiss that's as deep and long as the first one.

'Want to get out of here?'

'Hell yeah.' Liam grabs my hand and we dart across the roof to the door. Once inside from the wind and coldness of the downpour, Liam locks the door behind us, right as a crack of thunder roars in the air.

'You live alone, right?' I ask him.

He smiles his wide-dimple, soul-revealing panty-dropping smile. 'Yes.'

'Good, because I don't think Mike and Audrey would like me bringing a guy back to their house the first night I've moved in.'

Liam chuckles and pulls me under his arm as we make our way down the stairs. 'At the risk of freaking you out with the future thing, I kind of like to hope I'm the only guy you bring over to theirs.'

Despite my aversion to mystical matchmaking and marriage of time travel proportions, I kind of hope so too.

The rain eases up once we make it to the car, but a light drizzle continues to fall as we drive away from the planetarium. My clothes are stuck to me, and I shuffle out of my wet coat and crank up the heat.

Liam's townhouse is a five-minute walk from campus, but we drive over so my car is parked at his.

The sidewalk from campus leads right along his street, and on to an open pathway that would be the front garden in England. Only there is just concrete. Not enough space for a driveway, but it doesn't look like Liam needs a car when he lives this close to his work.

'This is handy,' I say.

Liam smiles and tries to hold back a laugh I can see brewing underneath.

'Oh, that's not what I meant.' I blunder. 'I meant for work.' I point behind us and his office a stroll away.

'I know what you meant. Just don't think that I'm some old researcher living on campus to pick up the students,' he says.

'You're not old.' I scoff. 'You're around my age, right?'

'Thirty-six,' he says. 'And that's old around here.'

'Jez, don't rub it in. I still think of myself as graduating a couple of years ago. It's a nice place,' I tell him on the driveway. It's a two-story new building with dark brown sandstone. Nothing like the student accommodation I stayed in at Newcastle.

'It's perfect for me. Close by to work and my dad's always in his office too, so we mostly see each other there or he comes here for dinner some nights he's working late.'

'You don't go home much? To him I mean?'

Liam opens his front door and shakes his head. 'Not anymore.'

The door opens right into the living space and the clean crisp walls match the walls and minimum furniture. I stand on the threshold, not wanting to drip over his perfectly clean home.

'Wow.' I look around the crisp white room. 'This is not what I was expecting.' Everything in here is chic and beautiful and nothing that looks like a single guy lives here. It's not a bachelor pad or students' digs. It's a home, a tasteful one at that.

'I'm not sure whether to be offended or pleased by that?'

I snort. 'Pleased for sure.' I unlace my boots to remove them before I stain anything. 'Wait—who decorated this for you?'

'I did,' he says proudly. 'Well, Stella's mom helped me. You know she's an interior designer, right? Well, I was one of her first clients. She never even charged me. She just took me shopping and helped me match up things I liked.'

'I like it.' I follow Liam into the room and lean over the side of the soft cream sofa and run my hands over the fabric. It's the right amount of soft feeling, with sturdy fabric, that I could run my hands over all day. The coffee table is small but perfect for the space and creates a great gathering atmosphere with the armchair opposite. Any more furniture in here and the place would be swamped.

Liam clicks the button on the fireplace and the gas clicks over, and the flames burst open and illuminate the room.

Despite the lack of personal items, the vibe is nice and intentional. Sleek. Liam walks through to the couches and toes off his boots at the rug. 'Make yourself at home.' He points to the couch.

Liam takes my coat and hangs it over a radiator. 'I'll get you some warm clothes.' He nods to the downstairs washroom. 'If you want to change in there. The dryer is in there too, so just pop your clothes in.'

I get to snoop around the downstairs of Liam's townhouse while I hear him opening and closing drawers upstairs. But there's not much to see or snoop. When I spin around, I see the only thing that gives away anything about Liam: his bookshelf. The wall under the staircase is an entirely purpose build bookshelf, bursting with all sizes of books. I can see no particular order from where I'm standing. Paperbacks and hardbacks, tall and shorter books all stacked haphazardly next to one another. It's the only chaos in the room, and I bet

104

the entire house. The open-plan kitchen space means I can see sheer white cabinets, and even his fridge magnets and shopping lists look organised.

I lean over the back of the couch to get a look at the titles on the shelf. Mostly they are science books and college textbooks.

'There's order there, I swear,' Liam says from behind me.

'I thought your place would be full of paper and research books, thrown all over the place, like a mad scientist on the brink of discovery.'

'Yes. Always thinking that he's nearly there. That he can't be disturbed, that he can't take an hour off.'

'Exactly.'

When I turn, he's changed out of his clothes into a white T-shirt and grey sweatpants. He hands me a pile of warm sweats.

'I used to be like that. For a good while. Until my dad saved me from the madness.' He chuckles, but I think he's being more serious that he wants me to know.

I stay quiet to see if he will elaborate.

'Pamela actually helped a lot more than just with the decorating. Having her and my dad come in and create a clear divide between office and home meant that I actually started thinking better. No work here.' He moves his finger around, showing the entire house.

'I have a laptop that I use for backup storage and rereading notes or checking online. But everything is in the lab and offices there.'

I nod along with him. 'I know how your whole life can be consumed by things. Every day, every minute. Every time you eat or walk or breathe, you're thinking and scribbling notes and ideas and theories you want to look into. More often than not, you end up going around in circles. Looking up the same things. Getting the same results. It's exhausting.'

'It is.' He tilts his head to look at me. 'But some things are too important to just sit around and wait for. That's why I'm hardly here. I come home late, sleep, and go back to the office early. I appreciate Dad's concern, and it helped to have a clear space I could come home to for a few hours but—'

'It didn't stop you from working.'

Liam shakes his head.

It didn't stop him from trying to save a version of me he saw years ago.

My insides are on the verge of confusion. I know this is the thing made for love stories, and I truly love the fact that he's been trying to save my life for so long. Heck, I fell in love with a version of him just like that, but I don't want him to want me because he always has. I want him to want *me* because of the person sitting on his couch right now. For the girl he just met and is getting to know. For the person he doesn't even know yet. But the pull and the lust and the goddamn clit-tingling smile he keeps giving me has me shifting in my cold, wet clothes.

'You're shivering,' he says. 'Go get changed, and we can heat up by the fire.'

I make my way to the bathroom to change. Liam's clothes feel nice on me. The softness of the underside of the sweats on my bare skin is thrilling and comforting in equal measures. I can smell a bit of his scent under the laundry detergent, and I pull the sweater up for a second sniff. Definitely Liam.

Our lives have been chasing and finding each other. And now that we have, we have no idea what comes next.

I toss my clothes into a ball and into the dryer and hit start. One thing I never needed living on the equator line was a

106

dryer. Five minutes of hanging clothes outside and your laundry was dried and aired.

When I come outside, Liam is in the kitchen and I follow him in. My feet chill against the cold tiled flooring. There's nowhere to sit in here. There's a breakfast bar but no stools, and a small square table and two chairs in the corner of the room. It's sturdy and expensive-looking, and matches the colourless scheme of the whole house, apparently. The only sound in here is the fridge humming, and even that is low. There's no background radio or neighbours TV that can be heard, and it's nice to have silence in such a cosmopolitan city.

'Drink?' he asks.

'Water, please.'

Liam grabs bottles of water from the fridge and gets two glasses and leaves them on the island. There is a whole marble slab between us, and it feels weird to have him this far away from me. I've spent years without him, but after that kiss, I want to touch him all the time. I guess to make sure he's real.

'I turned on the heat, so it will be warm in a few minutes.' He grabs his water, I take mine, and we return to the living space. On the walk back, Liam grabs my hand, and when we get back to the couch, he pulls me into his embrace. His heavy hand rests on my side, enhancing the feel of the soft sweats against my skin. It's thrilling. Having someone gravitate to you so early on. Not having to wonder where things are going to go after that kiss.

I look up at the bookshelf behind us now.

'I thought you would be more of a colour coordinating kind of guy,' I say.

'Oh god, no. I'm strictly a subject organiser. And by the amount of times I go back to things.' He points to the shelves that are the same height as the back of the couch and he lays his hand lazily on a book. 'This row here is the ones I want to

107

reread or reference. Don't even need to get off the couch to grab them.' He strains his neck and looks at the top. 'Those are important too, just not ones I search out in the middle of the night.'

I look around the couch and see the comforter and lamp are within easy reach too, and the couch is L-shaped, just the right size for Liam's tall frame to stretch out on.

'You're a night time reader?' I ask. 'Lounge around here instead of going to bed?'

Liam nods. 'More like an insomniac who needs to feel productive if he's awake. No point in lying in bed, not sleeping when I could do something like save my friends from some unknown time travel danger.'

I smirk at him and sip my water. 'It's relaxing here. I like your setup. Very Zen with the minimalist vibe.'

'Well, if you like Zen, you're going to love this.' Liam hits play on a remote control and speakers I never knew were around us play soft classical music. He gets up to the coffee table and pulls out a lighter and some Lavender+ candles. He doesn't even need to spin the metal jar around for me to know it's Lavender and Honey. I can smell it from here.

I take a deep breath and sit straight. 'Can I see that?' I ask.

'Sure.' He hands me the candle and tells me about the ethically sourced lavender in the African islands. I nod at him and turn the candle upside down, reading the label below.

'Not everyone realises that if you peel the label off, you get to see who made the candle. The farmhand who chopped the lavender, the worker who cultivated the oil and set the candle all have their names signed on the base.' When I peel back the sticker and see my signature with a love heart flourish, my heart sinks. Memories flood my vision and I have to push them back. 'See.' I tilt the bottom of the candle towards the light in front of him. 'This must be a year one product,' I tell him and hand the candle back to him. 'In the beginning, I did a lot of the work myself.'

'You worked for Lavender+?' he asks. 'That's pretty cool. What was it like?'

I smile tightly. 'The islands of Sao Tome and Principe were amazing. It felt like home, you know? I had been travelling for about six years by the time I found the place, and it was everything you could imagine from a tropical island. Breathtaking views, tropical weather, and heat right through to your bones, but the rain bursts helped cool the air when it was needed. People depended on the tourist industry, just like my family in Blackpool. I got a job in a hotel. In a small islet south of the main island, there is the equator statue, a national park, and a sister hotel of the main resort. I joined the population of seventy-five and worked as the check-in and tour organiser. Dan, the diving instructor, became my boyfriend, and we started Lavender+ together.'

'Let me guess, didn't end well?' Liam asks. 'I hope it ended anyway, right?' He tries to smile.

'It ended well, for him and his wife that he never told me about. The business was always doing well. I just never realised how well. I was always working the land and the house where we bottled and packed the products. He was the office guy. The money guy. Turns out he was sending it all home to his wife and kids, hiding the fact we were doing so well.'

'I'm sorry. That's a shitty thing to happen.'

I nod. 'He was happy to sell ethical products. He just didn't want to live his life with any moral standard. I think all our staff knew he was married. We were so busy that I hardly ever left the islet. He was the one who travelled for the business to make purchases and sales. It all made perfect sense

109

at the time. The night his family showed up, I left the island. I walked away from it all.'

I glance at the lavender tattoo on my finger that's starting to fade, and I can't wait until it comes off completely.

'Sorry, it was a long time ago now. It's just every time I see one of our products, the disappointment in myself comes back.'

'You hungry?' Liam asks. 'Let's order food, and you can tell me some good things about your life.'

'You first.' I feel his arm clench around me.

By the time the food arrives, I've already told Liam about Emmanuel and Isabela and their kids. How they not only gave me a job and indulged my crazy ideas for expanding the tour company. How their daughter roomed with me at the hotel she owned, and how I was brought to the family dinner table every Sunday and fell into the role of an adopted daughter. The trips we did for the company, the failed attempts at hiking deep into caves and inactive volcanos. And the places they refused to put on the tourist brochure but humoured me with a family trip to the Galapagos Islands, where Emmanuel and Isabela were not only originally from, but named their kids after. They were the experts of the group of islands and got us to cover a lot of ground for cheap.

Liam lays out the food containers on the counter, and I fill my plate with chicken and quinoa salad and a side of shredded beets. When we sit at the table and he takes his first bite, I ask him about his family. His childhood and how he got into research. Liam shifts in his seat and clears his throat. 'I know there's a raw nerve somewhere in your past, as you've avoided this conversation already. But if I'm all in trusting you, I need the same back,' I tell him.

His posture falls a little, but he looks up into my eyes. 'I killed my mom,' he says.

I freeze with my fork stuck in some food on the plate.

'It was an accident. I was obsessed with what had happened to me in England. I was having such a hard time figuring out why no one would believe me. I was trying to make some sort of machine in the backyard. It had poles and aluminium foil and all this crazy stuff. I didn't know what I was doing, really. But I had it hooked up to a radio and an extension cord running from the house. My mom was giving me hell about taking her metal colander from the kitchen when she was cooking dinner. She grabbed the colander and got electrocuted. I had been out there most of the day, and when it rained, I was too stupid to know to bring the electrical cords inside.'

'Oh my god, Liam, that's awful. I'm so sorry.'

I take his hand over the table, but he pulls it away.

'It's ok,' he says. 'It was a long time ago. And I'm making up for it.' He takes a bite of food, but it takes him an extra second to swallow.

'How are you doing that?' I'm genuinely interested to know.

'Me and my dad met David and he finally believed me. *We* decided we were going to figure all this out. That my mom's death wasn't going to be the end. That it wouldn't be in vain. After David came to travel, we knew there were other people who needed to be saved. And I think we're both hoping for a way to save her in the past, too.'

'Is that why you live here? So close to work, constantly punishing yourself by not having a life?' I ask.

'Well, you don't hold back, do you?'

I shake my head. 'Not enough time in life to dance around questions.'

'Isn't that the truth?' he says. 'And yes, it's why I live here. So I can work more. And I don't take vacations or time off. Even when I'm home, I don't like to spend too much downtime.

I guess it is a punishment. Why should I get to have a happy life? I need to do something important to make up for the bad things.'

I put my cutlery down, my mind spinning, and I accidentally stab my finger with the sharp knife.

I automatically hiss out the pain and pull my finger away. Liam is out of his seat to see what happened and we both have a chuckle at the tiny cut on my finger. Opening a cabinet, Liam pulls out the largest first aid kit I've ever seen. 'I think I only need a bandage,' I joke.

'I got you.' He unzips the kit and pulls out a small box of bandages. Sitting back at the table, he pulls his chair around to directly in front of me and opens up the wrapper.

'What's with the mini hospital?' I ask.

'I enrolled in an EMT course. Figures with all the events coming close together, and we have a fair idea that Audrey was injured the first time she travelled to Mike in the past, that we should have some medical staff close by.'

I nod. 'And you took that responsibility on, too?'

He smiles. 'It's more of a refresher. I did two years of medical school before I switched out to physics.'

'You really wanted to save everyone, didn't you?' I lean forward and run my hand over the stubble on his face. His long hair is tied back tight, exposing the short under cut and sharp jawline.

Liam still has my other hand in his, caressing the finger I injured. I move forward a little to kiss him. He wraps his arms around my waist and this time hauls me clear off my seat and into his lap. He stretches his legs wide, and I settle on his lap, right on his hardening dick.

I moan when I kiss him and grind down into him and gasp when he pushes up against my shallow thrust.

112

Our kiss is deep and wild and hungry. He moves his hands to my face, holding me in place as he nips and pulls at my mouth.

'Bed?' I ask and he stands, taking me with him in one clear movement.

'Jesus.' I laugh, nearly falling out of his embrace. 'No need to show off,' I tell him.

'Oh, there is plenty to show off.' He smiles and nips my neck as he carries me, straddling his hips through the townhouse and up the stairs.

I never noticed the rain start up again, but in Liam's bedroom it's the only thing I can hear. The pelting of the droplets off the window are strong and loud, and when Liam drops me onto the bed, the roar of thunder and flash of lightning through the window illuminates the whole room.

I laugh and pull Liam close to me. 'Close the damn drapes,' I tell him.

I'm already hot and would love to strip this sweater off me, but I'm naked underneath and despite asking him to bring me to his bed, I don't have the confidence to strip myself naked. Damn. I should work on that.

Liam pulls his sweater over his head on his way back to me. The tattooed, smooth abs attached to my long-lost supernatural angel pace towards me. Sweatpants riding low on his hips, muscled V-shaped waist longing to be touched and licked. I lean forwards and he grabs the underside of my sweatshirt and helps me lift it over my head.

'You've been naked this whole time?' he asks.

'Had to dry my underwear, too,' I tell him.

He grabs the pants I'm wearing, tears them down, and lets out a moan. 'My god, woman.'

CHAPTER
ELEVEN

The smell of burning lavender and the flashes of lightning behind my eyelids overload my senses, and I back out the door, onto the small dirt road. I'd recognise the hotel in Sao Tome and Principe in seconds, even in my dream state I know is taking over my subconscious. It's one of the weird things about being an anxious insomniac.

I know I'm dreaming, but I can't stop the hallucinogenic replays of my life.

I slowly bend my head back, facing the sky as the rainwater bounces down around me and splashes my face. It keeps me conscious and alive and breathing, and I scream. I scream to the dark sky and the universe and the unholy adultery god and let the thunderous storm roll over, echoing my angry cries. The lightning comes within seconds, not far behind me, and I run. Just like I always do. Around the back of the building, to the main driveway, I run into the storm. Not caring if the lightning strikes me down where I stand. But it doesn't. Instead, it strikes something more painful than my heart. The smell of my farmland burning half an hour south is bitter-sweet.

Smoke-filled lavender fumes cover the islet and everyone comes out to watch.

A few of the men follow Dan in a truck towards the fields, to do what, I'm not sure. But the rest of us watch my life burn. And I've never felt more relieved for the end.

I run to the beach, sticking to the dirt road, and wait until the forest is upon me on the west side. Thick trees and rubble are on this side, and in a storm, no one is going to chase me into the trees.

The lightning hasn't given up, flashing off the shore; the light shining, heaving through the thick shrubbery. Shadows cause a momentary panic each time the world lights up, causing me to stall and change direction. The wet moss under my feet becomes slimy on the broken branches and tree roots, and I slow down to not lose my balance.

The smell of burning lavender is lost, the further I go into the earthy smell of mud and moisture. The lightning stops, but the thunder continues raging around me.

I'm lost. Alone and heartbroken in a forest I should know like the back of my hand.

After about an hour of trudging around in the dark, I see light ahead and run towards it.

I throw my arms up in the air and shout out. Freezing from the rain that's soaked me and the crash of the last few hours. When I make it to the road, Dan opens the door and steps out of our truck.

Of all the people to come rescue me, I really didn't need it to be him.

The sight of him makes me tremble more. Who the hell doesn't realise their boyfriend of five years is married? Who the hell doesn't notice him smuggling out a million US dollars of funds from the business to his wife? I slide the plastic ring of lavender off my finger and drop it at his feet.

I don't have the energy to throw it. He and his lies are only worth being dropped on the ground. No more energy. No more feelings.

I slide into the driver's seat and close the door behind me. Taking off, I leave him on the side of the road to his wife and my business and my life and my dreams.

I wake up with a jerk in Liam's bed, and I can still smell the burning lavender from my past. I nudge a naked Liam next to me. 'Did you put out the candle earlier?' I ask.

He nods. 'Before we ate.' He's wide awake in only a second and he sits up, leaning his back against the bed frame. The frame he had me clinging to only a few hours ago. 'Don't tell me you wake up in the middle of the night worried about things you might have forgotten, too?'

I laugh lightly. 'Kind of. I've had really vivid dreams ever since I was a teenager, more like hallucinations. They used to freak me out because I could smell things and even feel things I touched in my sleep. The doctor told me it was a sleep disorder, so I let it go. They still make me anxious, though, like sometimes I need to get up and check that it was a dream. Sometimes, though, it's just a memory coming back to haunt me.' I shuffle up and lean into him, and he opens his arms and pulls the blanket tight against me. The rain and storm have passed, but there is a chill in the air, and it's comforting to have someone solid and warm to nestle into.

Liam runs his hand down my collarbone, across my chest, and the swell of my breast, tracing the heart tattoo on the side. The right breast has an infinity symbol in the mirroring position, making me the talk of all the parties I ever wear a dress to. Lucky for me, showing off side boob really made it popular.

'You want to go on a trip next weekend?' Liam asks. 'Think of it as a birthday thing.' He looks at me.

'That would be nice. Where do you want to go?'

'I know a place you might like. Let me make the plans?' he asks.

I turn away from him and close my eyes. 'That would be fabulous,' I say. It's been so long since anyone took charge of the planning and organising for me. So I sink back into a peaceful sleep, content with Liam taking over my life for a weekend.

This time, my dreams are peaceful. I dream of Liam's voice, talking to me through the tapes. But this time he's talking to me like we're a couple and we know each other. I can feel him in the bed next to me, and I can hear his voice chatting in the distance, letting me drift in and out of consciousness.

I spent the rest of the weekend with Mike and Audrey and the kids. I have no idea how they manage them every day. They constantly want to be entertained and be the centre of the conversations. It's been so long since I've seen them I don't care that they fight over who gets to sit next to me in the car, at the restaurants, have a colouring competition with. I'm totally in love with being the best aunt. Since Audrey's siblings still live in Ireland, and I've been gone most of the kids' lives, having a real flesh-and-blood aunt is a novelty for them. But I enjoy when Stella's son Max visits, and the kids torture him for a bit. Max is in the army, and even he has been home more than me. By the time Monday morning comes, I delight in having breakfast in silence in the tiny pool house at the end of Mike's property. A five-minute walk, and I'm in Stella's house. Despite David living across the street, he's particular about whom he lets work in his house. Most of his meetings go through Stella anyway, and I've been assigned to set up station there.

Max is coming out of the home gym when I enter the front door, and he gives me a sweaty hug as he passes by.

'Ew. Stop it.' I swat at him.

I have my ass in my seat and Stella beeps the outer office phone. 'You're late,' she says.

I look at my watch. 'It's eight thirty. Come on, don't be the dick-boss,' I joke and hope she takes it well. All our interactions over the past ten years have been via email and I'm worried she maybe has turned into the Iron Lady manager bitch the gossip columns say she is.

'Well, just as well you don't work for me.'

I smile.

'David already dropped off a box to take over to Liam.'

I chew on my lip and stop the smile from spreading across my face. 'Okay,' I say.

'Stop smiling,' Stella says.

'I'm not smiling. All I said was okay.'

Stella clears her throat behind me and when I spin in the seat, she's standing at the doorjamb with a shit-eating grin on her face. 'I heard you never came home from your date until late Saturday. That's a whole twenty-four hours.'

I try not to laugh and turn away from her. 'Where's the box?'

Stella nods to the legal file box sitting at the side of my desk. 'Try not to take your time. Liam's a busy boy.'

The box isn't heavy, and I can carry it back to Mike's house while I fetch my car. I should probably drive over here in the mornings, since I'm basically going to be an errand girl.

'Don't forget your security key card,' Stella calls after me.

Before I leave the office, I turn to Stella. 'I have a question. Do you know any international business lawyers that I might speak to? Someone who knows Portuguese law, maybe?'

Stella takes a minute to answer. 'Not that I know of, but I know a woman who could put me in touch with who you need. What do you need?'

118

'Just some questions about company law. I was swindled out of a lot of money, and I walked away from a business I built.'

Stella's eyes widen. 'I didn't know that.'

I shake my head. 'I never told Mike. Or anyone, actually. But I think I might be ready to get back what I built.'

'Okay,' Stella says. 'Email me over any details as you can and I'll forward it on.'

'Thank you.' I walk out the door, and despite the addition of the box file, I feel lighter than I have in years.

Getting through morning traffic from Beverly Hills to UCLA is enough to make me want to detour straight to the airport and hop on the first plane. I see why Liam lives so close to his lab. The stress alone must kill a million Americans a year. Their soul, at least.

I make it to the physics building and get the elevator down to the secure labs, where I have to use my key card to open the door to the hallway. I knock and wait for someone to come out of the lab to take the box from me, and when Ethan is the one I see coming through the glass doors, my heart sinks. I was looking forward to a glimpse of Liam. Maybe even a kiss, and to breathe in a little of him.

'Sorry to disappoint,' Ethan says as he takes the box from my hands.

I shake my head, pretending I don't know what he's talking about.

'Liam is in the teaching office if you want to say hello before you head back.'

I can't hide my smile, and Ethan directs me back up a floor.

119

Liam's office door is wide-open as I walk down the hallway, and I hear him moan in frustration. I chew my lip that I already know his moan from a distance and remember a much nicer, closer way I heard it this weekend. I pop my head around the door, and he's behind his desk, looking at a stack of papers. His head is held low, showing off his man-bun. His white-collar shirt is tightfitting around his biceps, and he has the sleeves rolled up, showing off the bottom half of his tattoos.

I knock on the door. 'I've got to say, the professor look has never been so sexy,' I say.

When he looks up and locks eyes with me, he smiles that lethal panty-dropping smile. 'Well, isn't this the best thing to happen this morning?'

I point to the coffee cup on his desk. 'I even beat the early morning caffeine fix?'

'You bet you do.' He puts his hand out in invitation and I cross the cramped room and lean down to kiss him in his seat. 'Good morning,' he says.

'Good morning. But I really preferred it when I woke up in your bed for a morning kiss. The drive over here alone would be enough to break couples up.'

Liam smiles. 'Well, I'm sure we could arrange for you to wake up at mine every morning.'

I like the idea of that, but the serious element of it makes me cringe.

'I meant that in a non-serious, completely taking things slow kind of way,' Liam says.

'As long as you're just using me for sex and I'm using you for accommodation, then we have a winner.'

Someone clears their throat behind us and Ethan is at the door. Fuck.

'Don't mind me,' Ethan says. 'I just wanted to let you know David sent over that piece you were waiting for.'

120

Liam jumps out of his seat. 'Can you?' he asks his dad, gesturing towards the stack of papers, and Ethan sighs.

'Yes, all right. I'll mark first-year essays. But you have to cook for me for a week.'

Liam taps his dad on the arm. 'Thanks.'

I follow Liam out of the office, but he's a fast walker when he's determined. I have to almost jog just to keep up with him, and when he gets to the elevator, and I'm a second behind him, he flinches like he forgot I was there. 'Oh god,' he says. 'Sorry, I need to go get this. But I'll call you later tonight? Tomorrow for sure if I end up staying here too late. I've made a booking for the weekend, so I'll let you know what to pack for Friday.'

Huh. 'Okay, no problem.' The elevator doors open and since we're going in the opposite direction, Liam enters and pushes the button for the lower level. He sticks his head out and kisses me on the cheek before the doors close and take him away.

I guess Liam in work mode is a totally different person than weekend-date Liam.

I've got to admire a man who makes his whole life a mission to figure out the wonders of the world. And a new work girlfriend isn't going to derail his attention. I can't figure out if I'm disappointed or not. Considering I'm part of the mission, now that I'm here, he's too busy trying to save me, to spend time with me.

When Friday night comes by, I pack an overnight bag. Bathing suit and hiking boots were Liam's instructions. I'm giddy with excitement at getting to spend the weekend with him. I only had to go over to campus two other times this week, and both times Liam could only talk for a minute before disappearing back into the lab. We spoke on the phone every night, but it was always late when he got home, and I could hear his voice drifting off and we would end the call. I think he sleeps on his couch most nights. In the dead of the morning, my alarm goes off and I quickly get dressed and make my way around the side of the house. Liam texts and lets me know he's at the bottom gate. I open the gates with the app on my phone and jog down the hill to meet him.

Liam stops the car when he sees me and gets out to take my bag. 'Good morning.' He smiles and kisses me on the lips. I want to linger some more, with his tongue on mine, but it's freezing, and I don't want to wake up Mike or Audrey. Liam stows my bag and I rush for the front seat. When I open the passenger door, the heat hits me and I sigh in relief as Liam climbs behind the wheel. 'Oh man, I was worried I would be freezing.'

Liam hands me a coffee from the centre console.

'You really think of everything, don't you?'

'Well, I thought since I was forcing you out of bed at five a.m., I might as well make it comfy for you.' He pulls the fleece blanket he keeps on his couch from the back seat and hands it to me. 'In case you want to get really comfy.'

'Don't mind if I do.' I bunch the blanket around my legs and busy my hands in the fabric. I'm not that cold, but I do like the soft touch. I kick off my boots and let my toes stretch out.

'Are you going to tell me where we're going?'

'San Bernardino National Forest,' he says.

I purse my lips at him. 'That's not far. Why so early?'

'Sun will be up by the time we get there. We need to hike to the springs, and it's best to get there before the desert heat becomes a problem.'

122

It's my turn to scoff. 'I can handle a little desert heat, you know.'

'Well, I know how much you hate traffic, so this way'— he grins—'we have the road to ourselves. Plus, I figured the quicker we get there and explore, the quicker we can get to the hotel.' He smirks.

I place my hand on the back of his head, circling my fingers around the back of his ear. 'You really think of everything, don't you?' I laugh.

Two hours later, we've stopped at a gas station for breakfast and arrived at the national park. The sun is out and our hiking boots are calling from the trunk. With the breeze light, I look up at the sky and take a deep breath. 'This is going to be amazing,' I say.

'I hope so.' Liam hands me my shoes and a water pack and I get ready. 'I really wanted to bring you somewhere that holds all your favourite things.'

'And what's that?' I ask.

'Adventure and nature. You like the outdoors and already told me you're an adrenaline junkie. Not much danger today, I'm afraid, unless you want to skinny dip.' He laughs. 'But I wanted to show you that you don't need to travel around the world to see the beauties and wonders of nature. We have them everywhere.'

I don't feel like I need to be moving, that I need to be exploring and finding the answers. I can relax here, with him, and enjoy the world I never thought I would live this long in.

Liam takes a small backpack out of the trunk and asks for my bathing suit. 'The hot springs are at the end of the hiking trail,' he tells me. 'I brought towels and lunch, so we'll be good for a few hours.'

It takes two hours to hike around the mountains and Liam sets a fast pace. We're quiet most of the hike, with only

123

the crunch of the stones under our boots. I'm glad for it. It feels freeing, like when I used to spend the weekends running in Quito with Emmanuel's son, Santiago. He used to drive me out to places and let me explore on my own while he met up with his friends.

The heat in the forest here, combined with the views of the mountains and the lake below, does exactly what Liam said they would. Remind me that there are wonders of the world on our doorstep. This early in the morning, the sun isn't strong, and the ants and lizards seem to sleep in too. Liam knows exactly where to go, and of that I'm glad. Years of making sure I don't get lost on hikes were fine, but over time, it made me anxious. What if that was the thing that killed me? What if I got lost and died in the elements? What if it wasn't something otherworldly or supernatural or time travely that killed me? Just plain old-fashioned getting lost.

I stop at a peak to get some water and look out at the lake in the distance. The clear water reflects the image of the tree line and the backdrop of mountains. It's still and calm and quiet and exactly what I need in life.

'It's beautiful. I never knew about this place.'

Liam stops next to me and I hear him catching his breath. We've been pushing it for an hour, and we're feeling it. 'Told you I had places I wanted to show you. And it's not just about the view either. I was thinking about what you told me about your trip along the equator line. And it makes sense about trying to anchor to the centre of the earth, or researching the core's electric charge current. But the meridian lines can be sliced anywhere in the world for a perfect centre. It's only the equator that is in a certain place.'

I nod. 'And even that moves.'

Liam smiles. 'Yes, it does.'

'Then why did you send me there?'

He shakes his head. 'I'm not sure, but there must have been a reason. I wouldn't send you on a fool's errand. Even if it was a different version of me from a different universe, there must have been something you needed to see or find. I think we need to sit down and go through your entire trip and locations. I need to know everything about how it felt and things you might not even have noticed at the time.'

'That's my whole life. It's going to take a while.'

'I know.' He takes my hand. 'But I'm not going anywhere, so we have the time.'

I take a deep breath. 'I need a minute.' I sink to the ground, cross my legs, and sit straight. I was never one for getting into a full meditation pose. I prefer to lie flat on my back for deep breathing, but the ground is uneven, so I stay seated.

I hear Liam sitting next to me, and I close my eyes.

'Sometimes it takes a minute for my lungs to fill. It's like I can't catch my breath, and I get palpitations. Blood pumping in my ears. It's all in my head, nothing wrong that I need a doctor. I just need to calm down.'

'I get it. There's a lot at stake here. It can mess with your head.'

I take a slow, deep breath in until I need to release it and take my time emptying my lungs. Over and over, I breathe in and out and Liam is matching my breathing. It only takes a few minutes and I feel like I can do this. I can figure out the world and what I need to do to survive.

When I open my eyes, I smile at Liam, whose face is soft and waiting for me. 'Thank you,' I whisper. Thank you for not judging me, for not thinking I'm crazy, for being patient. So many things I want to thank him for, but I can't speak the words out loud.

'It's all downhill from here,' he says, and I laugh.

CHAPTER
TWELVE

It takes less than an hour to hike down to the springs and hidden deep in the trees is a small dirt path that leads us to the edge of a small natural hot spring.

I'm sweating and sticky by the time we get there and I sigh out loud. 'Oh my god, I need to get in there.'

Liam drops his bag on the rock at the side of the bank. He's not complained about the bag once, and that's impressive, as I know how heavy even a small bag can feel when you've been on a trek for hours. He digs out the towels and bathing suits. He hands me my string bikini and I look around the trees. 'How the hell am I going to change?'

'There's no one here.' He strips off his clothes. I watch him lose his shirt and his muscles move and taunt as he bends to remove his boots and socks. He keeps eye contact with me as he undoes his belt and unzips his pants. I don't know if it's an invitation or a challenge, but I don't care. I'll stare at the man all day.

'What if people show up right when I'm naked?' I come to my senses and check behind me for anyone who might be approaching.

Liam chuckles and is down to his boxers, takes them off and tosses them into a pile with his clothes. He's naked for a full five seconds and he's teasing me with the time he's taking.

Slowly, he takes his swim shorts and puts them on. 'You know, I've no problem if you want to be naked.'

I shake my head at him and the bulge in his shorts. 'Really?' I mock. Picking up a towel, I toss it at him. Hold this at my back, will you?

With Liam covering my front and holding a towel at my back, I strip off and get my swim clothes on. There's no need for Liam to avert his eyes, but when I'm naked, he looks down and bites his lip.

'Something wrong?' I ask.

He shakes his head. 'Not unless you want a romp in the woods?'

Pushing him back slightly to put him in his place, the moment my hand makes contact with his bare chest, Liam drops the towel and grabs me. He kisses me fast and like his life depends on it. All I can feel is skin. His arms on mine, touching my back, my side.

He finishes his kisses by nibbling my lip and I totally want him to devour me.

'As much as I might like a *romp* in the woods,' I say, 'I'm totally getting into that water first.'

I walk past him and climb down the rocks, taking my time not to slip, with Liam at my back.

'First?' he says. 'Wasn't expecting that.'

'How deep is this?'

'You're good. You can walk in.' He takes my hand from behind and helps me step into the water. The heat over my feet is refreshing. The soothing balm travels up my legs the deeper I go, and I'm fully immersed in nature's wonders. I let my muscles relax. This is the best end to a hike I'll ever have. The cool air is enough contrast to see lazy heat trails drift from the water, like smoke. The water cleans off all the sand and dirt from my skin. I swim to the middle of the pool of water and dip

127

my head back, immersing my hair and scalp, and float on my back. The blue sky above me is interrupted by treetops and rays of sunlight shining through, as I slowly spin and move around.

When others come down to the spring, the serenity is over. A group of four loud, excited people join us and make conversation with Liam, who is near the rock entrance.

I stay as far away as I can, as long as I can, floating on my back, ignoring the world. I follow an orange and black butterfly that flaps above me. But I can't find my happy place with the chatter and clatter of opening cans of pop and sharing chips. It's bringing so much life into this place of beauty and nature that it feels all wrong. I enjoy being back home, with my family and friends, but I also want to be in the distant parts of the world with hardly any people.

The hotel Liam has us booked into is a casino resort close to the national park, and it's exactly what I need. A spacious suite with a large bathtub that I can pretend I'm still swimming in later if I need it. The bed is bigger than a king, and the sheets are crisp and beige and exactly like Liam's home. Liam places our bags at the door and locks the room behind him. Racing to the bed, he throws himself backwards and the bed bounces. I jump on top of him, my wet bikini soaking through my clothes. He strips us both and has my head hanging off the bottom of the bed before I know it.

'Can we just stay naked and order room service for the rest of the weekend?' I ask. 'I've had enough of people already.'

Liam is circling lazy strokes over the tattoo on my back and makes a noise in agreement. I love that he can't take his hands off me. I need to be touching him or feeling him all the time. It's only 2:00 p.m., and I know we said we would talk through my life's research and travels, but all I want to do is lie here and turn off my brain. The crack in the curtains shows the blue sky and I see a flash of light. 'Is that lightning?' I ask.

Liam sits up. 'Don't think so,' he says. 'Maybe it was a reflection from the lamp?'

I wrap a sheet around me, go to the window, look at the sky, and wonder.

'Have you any information about the weather and its effect on the earth's energy?' I ask.

'Not much, but we have some. Mostly it's about natural electricity and how to harness it.'

'Have you ever been hit by lightning?' I ask.

'That's such a specific thing to ask.' He squints.

'I was just wondering if someone can attract lightning more than others. It seems to follow me around, like there's always a storm brewing.'

'What do you mean follow you around?' Liam kneels on the bed, waiting for me to answer.

'I was hit by lightning when I was a teenager,' I tell him.

'So was I.'

Liam jumps from the bed and from his overnight bag, pulls out a notebook that's well-worn and half full of handwritten notes. He doesn't seem to notice, or maybe care, that he's naked and I have the drapes open. He flips to the first blank page he finds, writes something down, then picks up his cell phone.

'What are you doing?' I pad towards him, with the bedsheet wrapped around me, and try to sit on his lap. He moves his hands and lets me sit, but he has a voice recorder app open on his phone. 'When I was a kid and my mom died, the fire department said an electric current came through the

129

equipment I had out in the yard.' Liam leans forward, with his phone tight in his hand. 'But I swore to my dad that I didn't have any of the outlets plugged in. Everything was disconnected. The fire department insisted that there must have been a charge to run through the equipment, so when my mum grabbed the metal colander, it gave her the electric shock. I didn't tell them that I was fighting with her for the colander. I was holding on to the handle and I wouldn't let go. I didn't want her to have it back 'cause I wasn't done yet.'

'So how come you didn't get a shock?' I ask.

'I swear the electricity came from the sky. No one else saw the lightning, so I assumed that maybe I was confused.'

'But now you think it was lightning?'

Liam looks me in the eye. 'When I got home that night, my veins were bright blue, like someone had inked out their place in my body.' He shakes his head.

'Tell me everything,' he says.

We talk into the early hours of the morning. We order room service, and although it's convenient, it doesn't feel magical or romantic. It's a necessity.

I tell him about the early research I did and the ridiculous pamphlets I printed when I was a teenager. How the only person who would read them was the local librarian who kept and catalogued them for me in the system. I told him about my research on weather and thunderstorms and the types of energy they produce. About lightning theories and how they're monitored and calculated at different research facilities.

I tell him how I felt the buzz of electricity through my veins for years, and the small sparks of shock I used to create on the supermarket trolleys. How the energy readings I would take on my trip changed, depending on the time of day or the weather or my mood. It would take me weeks with copious sample readings to pin down what the energy levels might be without my own interference.

My theory on combining the natural elements of a particular location, along with the time of day, the earth's rotation, and the weather, along with the amount and type of energy a person had, all in the one place, might be different to someone else at a different time. And basically, there was no one magical place on earth. More like a combination of magical elements that all need to align together.

We've moved from the seating area, back to the bed, and taken a couple of ten-minute breaks. But Liam wasn't joking when he said he wanted to know everything. His cell phone ran low, and he charged it while we ate. His app ran out of space and he uploaded it to his email. I got a headache trying to recall every trip and every day and nuance of information from the last ten years of my life.

When I get annoyed and storm off to run a bath, he reminds me that time is ticking down to Mike's birthday. February is around the corner, and the 29th is the day Audrey is due to travel for the first time. And David too. Now that I'm here and alive in this timeline, Liam thinks something might happen to me too.

Liam bangs on the door. 'There's a reason we never had this conversation on the tapes I left you.'

I roll my eyes and crack the knot in my neck. 'I need a break, Liam. I'm not used to being grilled on this stuff. On having to justify my every move and thought.'

I fill the bath with bubbles and bath salts and let the water get piping hot. When I get inside the tub and my muscles relax, Liam strips off his shorts and slides in behind me. Supporting my back, I lean my head against his shoulder and close my eyes.

'I'm sorry.' Liam massages my shoulders and brings up some bubbles to caress over my skin. 'I just think that maybe I only gave you the information I knew, the things I learned, so that you could realise what your worth was in all of this.'

'What do you mean?'

'You're not just the messenger, Caitlyn. The progress you made on natural energy with lightning and thunderstorms, that's all you. It's not an area my dad or I ever covered. The thought of electricity having anything to do with this was just too close to home. I think we found a reason to focus our research somewhere else.'

'And together, we might have found out the right combination of things.' I realise.

Liam kisses me on the shoulder. 'How awesome is that? You were making so much progress all on your own, with no university funding or staff or friends to hear you ramble about your findings.'

'But I had you. Every time I felt like I was failing, I would listen to your tapes. I would hear your voice and keep going. That I was onto something.'

'David and I have made some progress with a time harnessing watch.'

I spin around as much as I can in the bath, and the water spills over the side of the tub. 'You mean like a time machine?'

'Sort of.' Liam tries to play it off cool. 'I think the electrical element is lacking. But maybe the weather or your theory on lightning might be an important part that we need.'

Liam wraps his legs around my waist and nibbles at my ear. 'I get sidetracked a lot by my work,' he says.

'I noticed.' I don't open my eyes when I answer. I just want to keep feeling the hot water over our combined bodies. 'I don't mind, though. I understand why this is important.'

Liam squeezes me tight. 'I'm glad. The last thing I want to do is ruin this between us.' He runs his nose over my face and inhales. 'I'm becoming a little obsessed with you too.' I can feel the smile break out on his face. 'And you're important. I just want you to know that I'm not putting you, or us, second.'

I clasp my fingers around the back of his head, grabbing onto his hair. 'You better not,' I tease.

'Is it crazy if I tell you I'm falling in love with you?'

I tense, although I try not to. He notices and pulls back. 'It's okay. I know it's crazy.'

'It's not crazy. I mean, obviously I'm adorable,' I tease. 'But I mean it. I'm totally falling in love with you too. But remember when we met? Oh, I don't know *a week ago*, and I told you we weren't getting married. We were going to take this slow.'

Liam chuckles.

'I said that because this is all going to come to a head in a few months' time, and I might not make it home. I might get stuck or die.'

Now it's Liam's turn to shift uncomfortably in the tub.

'I think I had a dream about us,' I confess. 'I always thought it was you, even though at the time I had only ever heard your voice on tape. But I had a dream that we were older, well, the age we are now, and travelling, and I was at the cave I'm normally in when I dream about dying, but this time you were there and I didn't feel scared. I recognise your tattoos from the dream.' I run my hand over his forearm.

'You had a dream about dying?'

I nod. 'I don't want to leave anyone behind if I die. I don't want to fall in love with someone so intensely that they feel the pain when I'm gone. I've been dealing with my impending death for years. And honestly, I'm okay with it now.

133

But other people might not be. And I don't want to leave you hurting.'

'Caitlyn,' he whispers. 'I'm so sorry I played a part in putting you through all this. I wish I knew why I didn't give you more information. I wish I could give you more. But know one thing, if you die, I'll be devastated, regardless if you tell me you love me or not.'

Liam grabs a sponge and lathers some soap into it and runs it along my spine. 'I think you've been preoccupied with your death that you might have forgotten how to live.'

'I've lived. I've done more than a lot of people older than me.'

'But you've never given yourself over completely to life. To love?'

I grab the sponge from him. 'I have now,' I tell him.

'Then move in with me,' he says.

I nod my head and shake it right after. 'You're even crazier than me. *We* don't even know each together.'

'Yes, we do. And if we had all the time in the world, we would take our time and, after a couple of years, plan a wedding. But like you said, we might not have more than a few months. And my biggest regret would be never having you in my life as much as possible.'

I bite my lip. I want to say yes. I want to be with this beautiful human more than anything in the world. It will be the most selfish thing I've ever done. It might hurt him when I leave, but damn, I can't help but be excited about the next few months waking up with him every day.

I nod as if I speak to say yes. I might burst into tears. The feelings are all too much. Too much excitement *and* fear.

I'm too damn selfish to say no. I hate myself for it. I hate myself for the betrayal I'll make when I'm probably going to die before our first anniversary.

CHAPTER
THIRTEEN

Los Angeles

My life feels like a series of time jumps. Like the things that happen in between aren't noteworthy. Since Liam came into my life, getting to know each other didn't take any time at all. It was like I've known a version of him my whole life, and it turns out, Liam here is exactly like I imagined him.

Every time he catches me smiling, he'll lean over and give me a soft kiss that always ends up with me opening my mouth and devouring him. I manage to contain myself if we're in public, but hot damn. When we're alone, I'm not sure which one of us ends up pushing the other down on the floor, couch, bed, or countertop. Kissing and touching and exploring have been my new favourite pastime.

We talk about our lives and our past experiences with time travel. We talk about Liam and David's research and what's happening with Audrey. The only person I've let listen to the tapes is Liam, and he's tried to interpret what he's said in like five different ways. He's sure there are reality differences for wherever this version of him is from, but he wants to make sure he isn't leaving anything uncovered.

The most concerning thing for Liam is the fact that in that version, I'm dead. And in the time travel experience Liam had, he'd seen a future version of me in trouble during a time travel switch.

We've made plans to retrace my research steps. Liam has promised David and Mike that we'll be back before the end of February.

He's booked the flights and arranged for accommodation and transport to give us enough time to explore and get on with the next location. We have three weeks to cover the ground that took me fourteen years.

When we get to the airport, he guides me and our luggage over to domestic departures. 'This isn't the right check-in,' I tell him.

Liam nods. 'A little stopover for a night before we get the long haul to Brazil,' he says nervously. 'Just a little precaution I wanted to run by you.'

'A precaution like what?'

'Marriage,' he says. 'Thought if we stopped in Vegas, we could get hitched, and you would have one more anchor to this world. One husband.'

I cover my mouth and try to stop the tears from falling. I'm both happy and excited and scared that we might not live through the next week to ever really enjoy a marriage. I want him, and I want to marry him. But I don't want to leave him a widower when I'm dead. The frog in my throat stops me from speaking, so all I can do is nod in agreement and I throw my arms around him.

Liam holds me tight and I can hear him as he breaths me in. 'Come on,' he says. 'Everyone is waiting.'

'Wait, what?' I shriek as he leads me to the check-in desk.

'Our families got to Vegas this morning, and some of your friends and family from England got in yesterday. Emanuel and his family couldn't come from South America, but they can't wait to see us when we get there next week.'

'Oh my god,' I whisper, 'you planned the whole wedding?'

I bite my lip and Liam squeezes my hand. 'It's small, just like I knew you would want it. There are like fifteen people coming. Nothing extravagant. But the ceremony is booked for tonight and we have dinner and music in the hotel. It will feel like a small family dinner.'

'Oh my god, did my mum and George fly from England with my dad?'

Liam tilts his head. 'Yes, but Mike already said that would be awkward, so he invited some family friends to come too, so it was more of a group thing. Your friend Natalie and her mother. Mike said that you guys used to be good friends, and she and her mom worked with your grandad or something?'

I chew on my lip. I've not heard from Natalie since she told me she never wanted to see me again. Hopefully she's gotten over the whole nearly dying on the beach thing with me.

I nod to Liam and cover up my sudden anxiety. 'It's been so long since I've seen them.'

Liam nods. 'I got to speak to her on the phone when Mike asked if I could invite them. She seems nice. She was a little taken aback about the invite. Kind of awkward on the phone. Hope it's not going to be weird having people you've not seen in a while there?'

I shake my head vigorously. 'It will be fine. At least there are another two people on the flight with Mum and Dad. That's the main thing. I would have hated for Dad to be stuck with Mum and George on his own.'

The smile splits over my whole face as the woman hands us our boarding passes.

'First class, for the bride and groom.' Liam winks at me.

137

'I can't believe we're getting married.'

'I can,' Liam says.

An arranged marriage on time-travel convenience isn't exactly romantic. Despite my reservations when I met him five months ago, I've fallen head over heels in love with Liam Bennett. And I would love to be his wife. To wear his ring and sleep in bed with him every night forever.

'It's not just for the anchor. It's for us. It's something I would want to do, regardless of all this.'

'You sure?' I ask him. 'Because if this all works out and I don't die, you're going to be stuck with me.'

I feel his heart beat faster in his chest, bouncing off the bones and vibrating through my own heart. 'I'm kind of counting on it.'

I scoff, like I always do when things get serious. A death sentence hanging over me most of my life, and the adulterous example of my parents' marriage hasn't exactly been a good influence on me.

'You know you should have applied for a licence to the chapel in Vegas if you wanted this to be legit. If it's for some feeling of belonging, I already have that—'

'I gave notice,' he tells me. 'We have the honeymoon suite booked for the night and a cab to take us to our flight in the morning. It's all sorted, apart from one thing.'

'What's that?'

'You.' Liam drops to his knees and pulls a brown shiny ring box from his back pocket. Opening it up, people around us stop and gasp. Someone cheers from far back, while someone else bangs into our luggage. Liam opens the lid to the box, and a gold engagement ring with a green emerald sits square and centre in the box.

I realise that the gasps are actually coming from me, as I sink to my knees next to him and pull the box from his hand. 'You got me a ring?' I choke.

'Of course I did,' he says. 'What kind of last-minute Vegas wedding would be complete without rings?'

'It fits.' I wipe the tears from my face.

'I measured a couple of your rings and the guy in the shop helped sort the size.' Liam turns the ring around and around on my finger, three times in total. 'For luck,' he says.

'I thought you didn't believe in luck.'

Liam swallows thickly. 'I never used to.'

'It's perfect.' And Liam is perfect for me. A last-minute, no-fuss wedding is perfect for me. And life beyond the next month would be pretty damn great too.

I nod instead of saying yes and throw my hands around his neck. 'Wait.' I pull back and look at him while I take the ring out of the box and slide it on my finger. 'You said rings?'

Liam taps his hand luggage. 'Wedding rings for me and you for the ceremony.'

I swallow the lump in my throat. 'I'd kind of really like not to die after this.'

'Me too.' Liam guides me to the gate, as I can't stop staring down at my new ring. It feels heavy on my finger, and I'm not used to the chill of the gold. But I love it.

My mum and Audrey get me ready for the wedding when we arrive. It's a flurry of activity. They brought a couple of short white dresses for me to choose from and have flowers and champagne waiting for me. There's a girl booked to do my hair and makeup, and all in all, I sit for an hour while everyone pampers me. Then I'm handed a bouquet and driven to the chapel around the corner.

When I see Liam waiting at the end of the aisle for me, I relax. I start to giggle inside at the craziness of getting married on the same day I got engaged, but I've been waiting my whole life for him, or a version of his to come and sweep me off my feet.

I don't pay any heed to the small gathering of people in the chapel waiting for us to say our vows and when I reach Liam at the head of the altar, dressed in a black tux, he takes my hand and I feel anchored to this world in a way I never have. I feel connected to the ground and the earth, like the anxiety that's always eaten away at the back of my subconscious is just gone.

I say a silent prayer to the universe that nothing comes in and steals us away from each other.

After the short ceremony, we walk down the aisle as man and wife, and I look out at our friends and family who are gathered in the seats. We stop at the end of the chapel and we greet everyone who has come to celebrate with us. I had already seen my mum and Audrey, but my dad and Mike are the first people who come and hug me tight.

'I can't believe you guys knew about this longer than I did,' I tell them. Everyone else is giving us some space to get caught up, and thankfully Natalie and her mum are chatting to George, so I don't have to hug either of them right now.

After a few minutes, the others, including Stella and David and Liam's dad, Ethan, join the small circle of chatter we have.

Mike ushers us all out to the waiting car service that's due to drive us back to our hotel and the private dining room that's waiting on us.

On the side of the road, Natalie approaches me finally, just the two of us, and gives me a tight hug. I squeeze her back, missing the years we've not been in touch. She was such a huge part of my childhood and my memories with Grandad.

'Hi,' I say into her hair.

Her voice croaks when she speaks. 'You guys look good together,' she says.

When we pull back, she is wiping her eyes, and I laugh at her. 'I never thought you were the cry-at-weddings type of person.'

She tries to smile, and her mum joins us. 'She's not, but she's been a mess ever since your new husband rang and told us his plan,' Sandra says as she hugs me. 'He seems like such a nice young man. His aura is all bright and sparkly.' She finishes speaking and turns to look in Liam's direction, who is standing with the boys at the chapel entrance. David has pulled out a box of cigars and all the men are holding one, not having a clue what to do with them since none of them smoke. I laugh at the ridiculousness of them all trying to look cool and my heart bursts with love for my family.

'He really is.'

'Natalie here keeps breaking hearts instead of settling down,' Sandra says and Natalie shushes her.

'I had someone important once, Mum, I already told you. Just because he couldn't stay with me doesn't mean I stopped loving him.' Natalie's cut short when Liam walks up to us and wraps his arm around my waist.

'Are we all ready to go?' he asks us.

Natalie looks at Liam without answering, and I can feel the awkwardness Liam spoke about earlier. I know she thinks there's something wrong with me. That I'm dangerous or something from that lightning strike on the beach, and the more I've learned over the years, maybe she is right. Is she

141

worried about my new husband? Surely if she thinks I'm too dangerous to be around people in general, she shouldn't have waited until now to spill the beans.

'People are never really yours to keep,' Natalie says to both of us. 'Trapping people in a marriage when they should be free to find themselves is not healthy for anyone, not now or in the future. We can't ever find the best version of ourselves if we're stuck somewhere.'

I look at Natalie, and she tries to shrug the comment off. 'No offence.'

I smile, trying to ease over the tension. I thought that the years of not being in touch would have healed a bit of our stupid fight. But maybe she's being catty on purpose?

'That's not really talk for a wedding celebration, now, is it?' Sandra says.

'Look around you,' Natalie says to the small group we have. 'Divorced,' she says to her mother. 'Divorced.' She points towards my mum and dad. 'Divorced.' She points to George. David and Stella are next on her hit list. 'Divorced.' And Liam's dad, Ethan, doesn't even escape the rant. 'Dead wife.' She says the last one a little too loud and gets the attention of the others.

'Natalie,' I hiss. 'What the hell is wrong with you?'

Liam shifts, like he wants to interject, but he's not sure of our dynamic.

'You never should have married him.' She is first to get into the waiting car, followed by her mum, who sheepishly looks at me in an apology.

Liam gives me a questioning look as we head to our own waiting car. 'What was that about?' he asks.

I shrug. 'I don't really know what's going on in Natalie's life anymore, but it sounds like she's bitter about love.'

Liam harrumphs. 'I get that. I felt the same way until I met you.' He leans over and kisses me, holding the car door open for me. 'It's strange. She was so different when I met her earlier.'

'Different how?'

He shrugs. 'She was nice.'

I sigh. 'I guess she never got over her whole *I'm dangerous* thing. She's got a point about love and marriage, though.'

'What's that?' he asks, settling in the seat next to me.

'All marriages end in heartache. There's either divorce or death. We're just too caught up in the moment to see it.'

CHAPTER
FOURTEEN

Ecuador, South America, feels different this time that I'm here with Liam. I'm over ten years older than since I was here last, and hopefully wiser, but it feels like I'm viewing the place with fresh eyes.

The drive from Quito International out to Emmanuel and Isabela's home is less than thirty minutes.

David and Liam have calculated, based on Mike's time of birth and Audrey's time travels to him over the last twenty years, that in two days, February 28th 2016 at 11:00 a.m. local time, here in Quito is going to be a significant time. And since I've dreamed of a cave in Quito and got stuck here all those years ago, this is a place I need to return to.

That is, if I want to be in a strong position so I can try to save myself from being pulled away in another timeline. And try to save David.

Liam doesn't want me to do it. He knows that this version of me here is safe, and deep down, he's willing to sacrifice the possibility that David might not wake up. He doesn't want me to risk my life. I don't really fancy the idea of it either. But if I can do this, I might do anything. And I won't be able to live with myself without trying.

Liam parks our rental next to Emmanuel's tour bus at the back of their house, and I jump out of the car. One thing I regret by following Liam's 'don't go back' rule, was never coming back here to visit. We call and Skype all the time, but it's not the same as an in-person hug. Isabela looks older than I remember, even from video calls, and she grabs me into a bear hug, shouting in Portuguese to the others in the house to come hug their sister. I love her for it.

I used to think my Portuguese and Spanish were excellent until I moved in with them. Originally from the Galapagos Islands, the family spoke both languages and refined my mistakes over the years. But they were delighted to practice their English with me, and even picked up on a touch of my accent before I left.

I introduce Liam. Cristobal, the youngest, is now a stretched twenty-year-old who grabs me in a bear hug and spins me around. I hold his face, so disappointed I've missed him growing up.

Santiago is with his wife, who I've never met, and their toddler, who wobbles next to his mama outside the house and I can't help scoop him into my arms for a hug. 'Where are Fernandina and Cruz?'

'Working, as always,' Emmanuel complains. 'What happened to taking life easy and having a family?' he says, and Isabela shoves him playfully.

'You know they won't stop working until that place is the way they want it.'

'That will be never. Those children are too fussy.'

'I wonder where they got that from.'

Emmanuel loves the fact his daughters own a tourist hostel.

Emmanuel pulls Liam inside and straight to the kitchen table where Isabela has dinner laid out for us. Despite two of their four kids not being here, the family is big and loud, and it was what I loved the most about my time with them. I hang back and Santiago puts one arm around me and the other around his wife, and we walk inside. Liam has wasted no time and is talking to Isabela about the Galapagos Islands and any local folklore that she might remember from her time being brought up there. I too had quizzed them about each and every place I visited while I was staying here, so I guess they know I've found someone who has a lot in common with me.

Cristobal wants to tell Liam about our family trip to the islands when they took me to visit the islands they were all named after, but Santiago has stories of his own about how he had to drive me around villages and hiking trails on our one day off a week. I give him a look and smile, knowing well that he enjoyed those trips where he got to drop me off at the nearest dirt trail while he went off chatting up the local girls. Many a time I found him in a bar, early evening, with a girl on his lap, and he wasn't happy about having to drive me home. Santiago must remember I know more about his adventurous youth than anyone else in the room and he drops the story he was in the middle of telling about me searching out every fortune teller and psychic on the continent.

The food and alcohol are flowing, just like a family welcome home party should be, and we exchange stories of my time with them in the company, and the hostel with the daughters. I glance at Liam, fitting in so well with my surrogate family, and I have to blink rapidly to hold back the tears that want to spill out. Tomorrow, Liam needs to fly home to L.A. and be with Mike and Audrey for the day that she starts time travelling. And I might not see him again. This might be the best and last day of my life. And for the first time, I'm truly terrified about dying.

146

I've changed Liam's flight, but he doesn't know yet. He only has another hour before he needs to leave, and it might be for the best, rather than dragging this day out.

We've driven out to the caves, on our own, where I first met Emmanuel on the tour and got stuck head first in a hole.

Standing at the mouth of the cave, the sun shining down on us, I hold my hand up to shelter the light, and the silhouette of Liam before me makes me dizzy. I must stumble, as Liam turns quickly and reaches out to grab my hand. His tattooed arms are all I can see, and the vision has come full loop. This is the thing I dreamed about all those years ago. When Liam was just a voice on a tape, and the idea of leaving Blackpool, even in the search of death, was the most appealing thing in my life.

'Are you okay?' Liam puts both hands on my shoulders, and the feeling is strong and grounding.

I nod. 'Now that I know I found you, after all this, it makes it worthwhile.'

'Don't say that like it's a goodbye,' he says. 'This is all going to work out. It has to. We've worked too long and hard for it not to work out.'

I touch the side of his face. 'It will work the way it's meant to.' I kiss him softly on the lips, wanting to be close enough to taste him, rather than anything else. 'I need you to stop in Blackpool before you go back to L.A.,' I tell him.

'I don't have time. I promised David and Mike I would be there in time.'

'I know,' I tell him. 'That's why I need you to leave now. Your bag is in the trunk, and I'm going to camp out here.' I unstrap the watch from my wrist—the watch David and Liam made and had me wear—and strap it on Liam.

'We're pinning a lot on hope. And I want you to have the best chance you can at making sure you get to where you need to be. David and Audrey and I are not the only ones who travelled through time. There was a version of you out there that started this all for me.'

Liam looks at the car behind him.

'I have you flying into Liverpool and a car for you. Find Natalie at the pier and tell her everything. I need her in on this.' I try to laugh. 'She was with me when I was hit by lightning on the beach when I was a teenager. She got pretty burned up hands from holding on to me. I think she might still have a part of my energy inside her. Get her in Johnston's pub at four p.m. for Mike's birthday. Just in case anything happens. She might see it or feel it or something.' I know I sound crazy, and I don't even know what help she might be, but I need to have all my bases covered.

Liam shakes his head. 'I don't want to leave you early. Why don't you call her and explain yourself? Ask her to go?'

'She won't talk to me. You saw how she was with me last week. She doesn't want me in her life anymore. I was a teenager and thought she was being dramatic about the accident we were in. But maybe she knew more than she ever told me. I think she met you before,' I tell him. 'She gave me the tapes you recorded. She told me she found them in my grandad's fortune teller's cabin. But I think she knew more. I think a version of you gave her those tapes twenty years ago, and she felt guilty when I began to live my life by them. There was a version of you out there I kept trying to find. Kept trying to compare every guy I met to. But he was never mine. I think that other version of Liam was only ever going to be a guide for me. Maybe he has other plans for his life, but he gave them up to help me. You, however, you are the one who was always mine. As soon as I met you, I just knew we were meant to be together.'

I pull his hands from my side. 'This is the last thing I need. Ever since I met you, you've been protecting me and trying everything you can to make sure I stay alive in this reality. But it's time to let me go and save myself. Regardless of what happens, there needs to be a reason behind it all. And we won't find out what it is until we return. All we know so far from a future version of Audrey and David, and even you from an alternative reality, it all stops tomorrow. We haven't had anyone beyond that date come to us in the past,' I tell him. 'David and you have been putting so much focus on tomorrow and how that is the day that starts it all and everything that's ever happened to us. But I want to know what comes next. That's the future I'm interest in, the future we know nothing about. And I'm scared I might not get to see that day if I don't work through this time loop that we all seem to be stuck in.'

He nods. 'I'm scared,' he says. 'I'm just scared I'm going to lose you.' Taking deep breaths, he's trying to hold back tears.

'Neither one of us is ever going to be truly gone. We're going to be living in past versions of this entire thing. You need to let me go.'

Liam's eyes snap up to mine and there is anger there.

'If I'm meant to die, then you can't change that.'

'Then what's the point?' Liam yells. 'What's the point in getting this warning, if not to save you?'

I let my shoulders drop in defeat. 'To meet. Maybe these last six months were the most we were ever going to get. And I'll take that every time over dying without ever having you in my life.' A butterfly lands at our feet and sits there for a minute, as we both look down and absorb this surreal moment.

When I look at Liam, he's not as awestruck as me. 'You know that butterflies symbolise transformation and rebirth.' My insides are calm as I look between the butterfly at my feet and Liam. Knowing that this is the sign I needed to push Liam away and follow the path we've been on.

'I need you to trust me and respect my decision.'

With one last kiss to the head, Liam releases me. 'I'll see you soon.' He walks to the car and drives off, and I watch the car go into the distance long after I can't see it anymore.

Eleven a.m. local time is Mike's birthday and when Liam and David think the time travelling begins for Audrey. Natalie agreed to be in Johnston's pub in England at 4:00 p.m., and Liam should land in L.A. about now. I have hours before eleven o'clock, but I've hardly slept all night.

Camping out sounded like a good idea, but it's been too long since I last slept in a tent and my body is older than I remember. I tossed and turned most of the night. The small rocks under the surface of the tent felt like boulders after a short while. Cracks from the campfire were comforting at the start, but when the flames died down and the sounds of critters and animals mixed in with the crack and pop of the wood, everything became a little scary on my own.

At first light, I'm awake and out of my torture bed. I scramble out of the zipped entrance and my body stretches back into place. I can still smell the smoke from the embers of the fire, and it makes my stomach grumble with thoughts of food. The sunlight across the desert dust is soft for this time of day, and with no one around, I'll calm my mind with some morning yoga. No point in going cave exploring with stiff aches and pains. The only sound is the tent gently flapping in the breeze and it helps calm my breathing and heart rate.

Once my morning workout and breakfast are complete, I pack my backpack with my phone and charger, a bottle of water, and a protein bar. The rest of my tent and supplies can stay here. I won't be needing them either way.

I follow the same path I did all those years ago, down the steep incline and past the cave markings that meant so much to me the first time I came out here. As the pathway gets darker and I use my phone for light, coldness comes over me. Liam and I went over all my travel destinations and I always kept coming back to this place. The place I always thought I was dreaming of when I had nightmares of being trapped. The place I thought I saw a future version of Liam and myself at. For me, this was the place I could connect with the earth. I've been further and deeper below sea level in concave volcanoes and underground compounds.

But here, I always knew there was an aspect of the light spectrum that I could not see. That if I could get in the right place at the right time, and the conditions were right, I would be able to see those swirly green and purple lights. That I might save myself or a version of myself. That the connection or anchor I needed was my determination and the power inside me. That maybe I was the one who held the energy needed to connect to the centre of the earth. That at the right time in the shift of the universe and the leap seconds that Liam and David have been researching, that I might just be the phoenix I've been searching for all along.

When I arrive at a fork in the cave, I forget which way Emmanuel brought the tour group and end up taking the wrong path. I need to double back. On the way, I drop my phone down a crevice and eventually hear it connect with water below. I curse out loud. My eyes have adjusted a little to being in the darkness, but I need to take small steps and feel my way back along the wall to the other entrance.

With the darkness, I can feel my breathing become harsher as I try to adjust to the idea that I'm searching blindly for something that is either going to kill me or save my life. A twig cracks under my foot and I scream.

I wait a second for my heart rate to come down and keep moving.

Once I think I'm back on track, I realise I can see more than I thought when I pass some markings on the cave walls. Drawing and symbols left behind from ancient times. It feels disrespectful to be touching my way across them. I follow the drawings of men with spears and fighting with wildlife. The symbols of marriage and birth. Of storms coming to destroy land and the men seeking shelter in the caves until the gods had calmed.

I become engrossed in the story unfolding before me, that I speed up my pace and I'm upon a family of bats suspended from the ceiling, sending them into a fury flight, screeching to alert the others to the danger. I try to hold still and hide my face from any scratches or bangs from their wings in this tight space, but they can't find a way past me. The force of them flying around me makes me lose my balance and I trip, smacking my head into a jagged corner in the process. I land on the ground. My hands land in a pile of loose rocks and dirt. The bats have space to fly and I hear the flaps of their wings in the distance as they make haste. Wiping my hands on my pants, I shakily lean on the cave wall for support as I pull myself up, and it gives way under my weight. Or maybe there was no wall there at all. It doesn't matter, but it's all I can think about as I'm free falling. It's a minute before I hit the ground.

I don't know if my head hurts because I banged it again, or if it was just the rock that has me feeling dizzy, but when I lift my hand to touch the side of my head, it feels wet and I know it must be blood.

I'm too dizzy to sit up, but if I stay lying down I might just fall asleep. So I roll to my front and slowly drag myself to the side. It takes a few minutes before I feel something hard and I use it to prop myself up. Sitting up is a new luxury and all I want to do is catch my breath and go back outside. I don't know what time it is and where I'm supposed to be. But maybe I can start from the beginning again and find my bearings.

My head feels heavy and when it jerks down and I get a fright, I know I must have fallen asleep or been about to doze off. When I look up, I see the lights. Green and yellow lights in the distance, getting stronger and closer. I wait until I have the energy and roll myself over. Clutching my backpack, my only possessions left now, I wait for death to come for me.

But I'm not that lucky.

I have things to do first.

The crack of blue light cuts right through the peaceful green swirls and electrifies the entire cave, and me inside it.

PART THREE:

THE END.
OR THE BEGINNING.
WHO CAN REALLY TELL?

CHAPTER
FIFTEEN

I don't know how Audrey moved through time so much. The Audrey I know from my timeline hadn't ever time travelled before. It's tricky like that. On Mike's fortieth birthday, his wife woke up thinking it was an ordinary day. Had no idea that by the afternoon she would have experienced her first and twentieth time-travel experience.

For Mike and David, Audrey has been visiting them for years. They're so used to time travel, it's a part of their past. But when you're the one travelling, you have no idea that in a few hours you'll be an entirely different person.

By now, if the timelines add up, Audrey will be hurtling back twenty years in the past to begin this loop all over again.

Audrey experienced a serious head injury in a car crash, at the right time, at the right place, that caused her travels. Each year, getting closer to going home, getting closer to her injury, that they wondered what awaited her when she returned to her time. To now.

I'm worried about her. I'm worried that David and Mike said the last few times she came to them in the past, her injury was more and more prominent. I'm worried that this is just the start for me.

When the light show in the cave seemed to heighten, I could feel the lightning in my veins. I've always had twinges of

155

the memory of what it felt like the night I was struck. The night Natalie and I were thrown into the air and tossed onto the shore like an empty crisp packet left behind by one of the tourists who don't give a shit about cleaning up the beach.

We flew into the air, weightless and loose-limbed, flailing around for what felt like an eternity before the wind moved us along a few feet and gravity pulled us down. It was the pain on impact that made me scream. The electricity heating my blood. Scratching to get to the heat in my dermis. Not being able to ease the burn inside of me. Natalie, once conscious, was hysterical about knowing the future and how she should have seen this coming. It was like the electricity fried her brain, and she believed in all the ways she faked the tourists at the pier to make her living.

But what if she was right after all? What if she could see the future and she knew all along that I was cursed? What if the two-week stay in the mental ward for rest wasn't warranted after all? What if her reputation with the locals hadn't ruined her business?

The free fall from the cave floor feels like that tossed crisp packet on the beach, and I know the landing will be my undoing.

Colour comes into view from the darkness.

Not the green swirls of the aurora lights. But of people and buildings and cars. Sunlight and blue skies and everything hits me at once. I'm falling face down, though time has shifted and slowed on my approach. I splay my hands to break my fall, and sparks of electricity jump from my body to the ground, and I bounce on impact.

I roll over and moan. Taking in the sights and smells of a back alley. Grey concrete, stained brown and yellow. Oversized metal dumpsters that I've only ever seen in America, and the smell of urine and hot steam. Looking at the sky, half of my vision is blocked by a high-rise on one side. Glass windows and brown bricks tower on one another like a concrete layered lasagna.

I get up swiftly, and the leftover pain from the sparks of blue energy isn't as bad as I thought. The day is bright, despite being behind a dampened building, and the writing on the trash cans is in English. A wall of dumpsters in various colours, including a yellow one labelled up hospital waste.

A loading dock door is open to the side of the building, and instead of taking a walk around the front of the street to see where I am, I'd rather sneak around the back and investigate why I fell here, of all places.

The side door brings me through to the ambulance dock. I pass by the staff room, and in true TV style, make a dash for a locker that's partially open and look for some clothes. If I'm where I think I am, I might have to hang around. And in my shorts and tank top, I'll be mistaken as a patient or family member.

The first locker is a guy's and I grunt in frustration. I try all the handles and after a few, one of them opens and I find black pants and fresh socks that will fit me. A sweater is dangling over a chair of the grubby excuse for a staff dining table. No wonder no one is eating in here. The place is small and cramped and not one bit relaxing in the middle of a fourteen-hour shift. I roll my shorts up and throw them in the trash. The sweater is too small and tight, but I squeeze into it anyway and grab a clipboard to carry around with me. Keeping my head down, I walk towards the crowded hallway.

The clock on the far wall reads three-oh-six, and by the darkness outside and the drunken, bleeding patients and tired-looking family members, it must be three in the morning.

I wonder if there were no drugs and alcohol in the world, how quiet the hospitals might be. No bar fights or drunk driver crashes. No intoxicated partygoers falling down stairs or accidentally setting their kitchen on fire. No card games getting heated and ending with stabbings on the highway. That's what I'm looking for. What Stella told us about David dying in her past. And where I hopefully am.

The early nineties aren't something I remember well, being that I was around ten years old. But the clothes and technology certainly fit this time period.

People here are wearing Shell suits instead of sweats. White washed denim jeans and jackets. Big hairstyles and multi-coloured sweaters. Thick back TV bolted to the wall with a coin operator is currently a blank screen, whilst a radio crackles low music in the background. The only thing that can be heard over the whispered conversations of the injured and their loved ones. Stacks of paper charts lining the desk with one old-looking PC to run the whole ward.

I smile at the two young kids sitting next to a woman who, I assume, is their mother, waiting. They are slumped to her side, but each has their own Walkman and wire headphones over their heads. Orange fuzzy earpieces only drown out some of the sound of the music, and it reminds me of how all this started. Tapes and a Walkman I kept well beyond its technological advances.

A few newspapers litter the empty beat-up seats in the waiting room, and that alone is a sign of past times. I can't even remember the last time I bought a magazine or didn't get my news from my phone. No one here even has a phone in their hands, let alone is absorbed with it. No social media check-ins at the hospital, or selfies with their friends' wounds. Cell phones weren't popular in the '90s, I remember, but I would have thought a few people would have had them out.

I lean over and intrude on a conversation between a patient waiting to be seen for what looks like a leg injury covered in blood and his mother. 'Is that today's?' I ask, pointing to the abandoned newspaper next to them.

'Yes. Well, yesterday's now.' She hands me the paper and I thank her. I dodge the abandoned Styrofoam cups, balancing with dregs of cold coffee on the table and edge my way around the seating area. An old man with two black eyes, a young woman nursing her arm, face contorting in pain, and two guys who look like they were in a fight with torn shirts and blood staining their faces and hands all avoid eye contact with me. I follow the arrows that point in direction of the wards. Passing through the double doors, I glance at the date stamp. Friday, September 24th 1993. So it must be the early hours of Saturday morning. Just like Stella said. David was stabbed on the highway last night and his body was found during the night. He spends a whole day in the morgue—dead, presumably, before the body goes missing.

As a young woman, with no knowledge of time travel or who David would become to her in the future, she thought her ex-boyfriend, the guy who killed David, had somehow stolen his body to hide the evidence. It filled the next years of her life with even more fear of what her baby dad could really do if he ever came back into her life.

But Liam and David now think that there was time travel intervention. And since I went missing in one of their future timelines, they really hoped I somehow made it here to this day and stole David's body.

Part one. Check. Make it to Los Angeles in 1993. Not sure how I did it, so not confident enough that I can leave or stay as long as I'm needed.

Part two. Steal a dead body.
Part three. Bring him back to life and back to 2016.
No sweat.

How I managed to not only time travel, but location travel is a little freaky even for me. This is clearly Los Angeles, a mere three and a half thousand miles from Quito.

Lingering in the hallways, reading the nothing on my clipboard, I know when David is brought in.

John Doe, DOA. Mid-thirties to forties. Stab wound to the abdomen. Found on the highway.

The EMT rattle off transfer to the doctor like they were reading a menu. I glimpse my friend, dead on an ambulance trolley, being wheeled past me, and I try not to flinch. Try not to gasp or hold my breath. Try not to believe that it's really him. That he's really dead.

The doctor brings David into a curtained area and calls time of death. He is with David for a few minutes, and I peek through the gap in the curtains as the doctor fills in some paperwork and hands it off to the nurse.

Seeing David's body being transferred from the hospital downstairs to the morgue is really creepy. And sad. The grief hits me harder than I expected. I knew it was going to happen. I knew he was supposed to be in an accident in the past, which has triggered some sort of coma in the future I left. But knowing is one thing. Seeing your friend die is just sad, no matter what timeline you're in.

Mike being in the movie industry has certainly paid off, and sneaking around a hospital really is as easy as it looks on screen.

You don't even need to steal a lab coat. All you need is a stethoscope. Roll up your sleeves, and a little tired looking and you'll pass for an overworked junior doctor. Well, I'm thirty-six, so maybe a junior doctor is pushing it.

An ID card attached to a laminate, facing the wrong way, and no one even asked to look at it.

I move around the hospital most of the day, like I was supposed to be there. Hiding in various empty rooms and moving on before someone became suspicious. I've not eaten all day and never noticed until someone left a half-eaten sandwich and coffee in the coffee shop. I swiftly sat at their table and read the newspaper until I felt it was safe from people noticing that I was about to devour someone else's leftover tuna.

One thing the movies got wrong is that a morgue is not an abandoned lab. It's a working environment, not allowing people to move freely unchallenged.

I keep walking the full length of the corridor and note the rooms on either side, and the direction signs above my head.

I count six doors, with staff behind each door. One looks like an office, with two staff members at desks. One is a storage closet, and one doesn't have a sign or window on the door. The other two doors at the end of the corridor are where they house the bodies. Both doors have electronic locks and are sleek glass doors that allow for people to see what goes on behind the doors. One doctor is on the move with a trolley from one room to the other adjacent room as I pass through the hallway, towards the exit door at the end. It must be the room they do their autopsies in and record their notes.

When I push the exit button and get out the other side, I keep walking up the stairs and through the main hospital again.

The office staff will be there at least until the end of the working day. Hopefully, the night will be when the morgue staff are gone. I'll need to find a place to change clothes again. The doctor got a good look at me, and passing through the morgue doesn't feel like the routine of a hospital doctor.

I've never stolen anything in my life, but I need a key card to get access to the room they keep the bodies in the morgue.

The only plan I've come up with is to get it straight from a doctor. Spilling a cold cup of coffee over someone is the best plan I have. It was how I got my wallet stolen once, and it was the best distraction tactic that's ever worked on me. At first, you get the shock of waiting to be scalded by the coffee, and then pure relief that it was cold and the only damage is to your clothes. Those precious seconds of redirection are all it takes not to notice the feel of your belongings being taken from you.

I sit in the hospital coffee shop at the main entrance and wait until I see the doctor from the morgue leaving. One good thing about Mike dating a nurse for years was listening to her talk shop. The hospital shifts always ran late, and the 8:00 p.m. finish time was never a guarantee. But it's given me something to start with. I've been around all day, but my serious stalking begins now. Fifteen minutes is all I have to wait for. I guess working on the ward where your patients are already dead means there are no emergencies that can't wait until tomorrow. Let's hope there isn't a fully staffed night shift.

I slip out the side exit of the café, into the hustle of scaffolding from the building works outside. The loud machinery working in the background will help with my act that I can't hear properly if anyone tries to stop me, and walk briskly towards the front entrance, ready to bump into the doctor on the way out. Switching the coffee cup to my left hand leaves my right free to grab his security card off his belt. The construction workers outside, combined with the patients and hospital staff, make the entranceway feel crowded. Perfect for what I need.

I run into the doctor with more force than I intend to, and the shock on my face is genuine.

The bang has thrust us both backwards a step and I grab the key card when the cold coffee soaks his shirt. We both gasp and I apologise as I bend down to gather the fallen coffee lid and slip the key card into my pocket.

'I'm so sorry,' I shout. 'I got beeped, and I wasn't looking.' I back away, people stepping between us, trying to get past. A great visual barrier I wasn't expecting. 'Leave your name at the ER, and I'll pay for your dry cleaning.'

The doctor huffs out his frustration. 'It's okay. Go,' he yells after me, allowing me to respond to my fake-emergency beep.

CHAPTER
SIXTEEN

I've never seen a dead body, let alone been in a room full of them. There is a chill in the air that might entirely be of my own making. Granted, the bodies are all out of sight in the drawers that you would expect, but it doesn't make the knowing any less real. Three high, and ten rows of metal mini doors that fridge the recently deceased. There are numbers on the handles but no way to identify who is inside.

I'd rather avoid opening thirty drawers of the dead to find David. There are charts on a file holder on the wall. I pass the deep steel sinks with hoses attached to the taps and pretend I didn't see the metal instruments and hanging scales stored at the side. There are wall units with glass doors that are labelled up with things *like evidence bags* and *human waste*. Right next to a box of biro pens and latex gloves. A stationery hoard for psychos.

Each slot on the file holder on the wall has a number, and I look through the John Does. There are two. Adrenaline pumps through me. Drawer number seven and eleven.

The first one, seven, is the closest, and I pull it open and find David. Relief swells through me that I have him, but some disappointment that there is no one to find the other John Doe. No time travelling universal spinning magic to cross time and space to find a missing friend. Not even a name to claim him.

It makes me sad to think that someone else is lost in death. I leave David and pull open drawer number eleven. The thing about a dead body, I've learned now, is that they look like a shell? Like a body that has no person or personality inside. 'I'm sorry,' I tell the man lying before me. Sorry for what? I'm not entirely sure. But sorry that he doesn't have someone to claim him. I click the door closed and look at David on the trolley.

How the hell am I going to get him out of here?

Luckily, like I hoped, this ward down here is empty of staff this time of night. But it's still early enough that I could raise suspicion moving around. I go to the room opposite, key card letting me in, and take a gurney back to David. Jessica was right. Being a nurse or doctor or hospital staff member is tough on your back. Moving people and equipment around is heavy work.

I take five minutes to get the gurney to the highest point, parallel to David's drawer. I grab onto the sides of David's shirt and use it as leverage to slide the top half of his body over to the gurney. Followed by his legs and feet. I have to stop and shift his torso over and hold back the tears at the coldness of his body. I realise that since he's fully dressed, they didn't start the autopsy yet, and the realisation makes me choke out a tear-filled scream. I've no idea if we can save someone who died in the past, but the thought of him being cut open if I was too late is enough to unravel me.

I say a silent prayer that we are on the home stretch. I've got him. Now I just need to get him out.

♡₊˚⟡˚₊♡

The only place I've ever seen a time travel wormhole open and active was in a cave in South America. In my dreams.

165

If Liam's theories are correct, there are cross dimensional wormholes all around us. Leap seconds and time recording have created so many blips in reality that we are literally surrounded by missing time. The only thing that Liam and Ethan and David ever truly struggled with was trying to activate it. Hell, even Carl Wilson, who literally wrote the book on time travel in England, never had that kind of theory. He was all about building machines to manipulate electronic disruption. I think he only ever wanted to interview me on my theories on time travel to prove himself right, rather than get any actual helpful views for his book.

Getting the whole way out of the hospital is my first step. My heart is pounding in my chest as I wheel the trolley out to the hallway and turn the bed to the right, towards the first set of doors in my way.

Manoeuvring this is harder than it looks. Once out in the corridor, there is a lift at the end, which is the back of the hospital. It stops on all floors, but it is out of the way that patients aren't going to be running into dead bodies too much. Now that I think of it, even in the hospital I've never seen a dead body being wheeled past me.

I need to get one floor up to street level and then find my way out from there. The buttons at the side of the doors are well-worn, and I squint as I push for street level. The faded background illumination lets me know my selection has been activated.

In the elevator, the doors close and I close my eyes and take a deep breath as the lift shudders on its ascent. The bright fluorescent light above us flickers and the start of a headache is coming my way. It's been a long-ass day.

I place my hand on David's cold, tacky arm. 'Hi,' I tell him. My arm brushes off the metal bars of the gurney and the tiny spark of contact makes some complete combination of the right time and the right circumstances.

The lift comes to a halt on the floor, but instead of the doors opening, darkness hits us for a second and the free fall begins. I cling onto David's cold arm to keep him next to me. Now that I've found him, I'm not letting him go. My feet never leave the floor beneath them, but the pull is the same as falling a hundred stories. This time I land gracefully, rather than being spat out of hell, and the lights come back on.

Only it's not the lights in the elevator or the elevator we are in anymore. The stale smell of antiseptic is gone. The tactile surface I wheeled the bed onto is gone. The tight box, the lights, the automatic doors have all disappeared. Or maybe it was us.

I look at the trolley and David under the sheet, my hand sparking blue light. We're in a dark room, with nothing surrounding us. It's anticlimactic. I wanted it to be more dramatic and fulfilling. The natural and manmade phenomena of the world I've been chasing for half my life have been beautiful and big and otherworldly. A lightshow near the equator. An underwater cave glowing green with sand sinking through a hole in the rock bottom, making the entire lake appear to be falling into a waterfall. The rapid rising of the sun behind a mountain and casting a yellow glow on the statue of Jesus in Rio de Janeiro. Snow on Volcan Cayambe, one of the hottest places I've ever stayed. Cracks of lightning breaking twenty feet before me and standing to tell the tale.

Time and dimensional travel, apparently, is simpler. In a split second, or so it *seems*, you've moved realities.

There is a calmness here that I always seek in meditation. Stillness, blackness, and silence. It would be calming if I had brought us here intentionally.

I spin around to see if there is anything I can grab onto, walls or doors or even a sense of location, but there is nothing.

When I turn back, the gurney and David's body are gone. But I can see a window in the distance. It started out small, but is slowly growing a few feet in front of me and finishes the size of a police interrogation unit. Maybe I got shot by an American cop for stealing a body, and now I'm being arrested? Some part of me is having an out-of-body experience. I take a tentative step forward, but I hear a voice behind me that makes me jump.

'Caitlyn?'

I turn and David is in front of me. Fully clothed and no longer dead. 'What the hell is that?' he asks, looking at the window over my shoulder.

I spread my arms and throw myself at him. 'You're alive,' I whisper and squeeze the life out of him.

David looks at the darkness that surrounds us, and his focus lands on the window the size of a wall.

'I always wondered if this place existed,' he says.

'You know where we are?'

'Black hole,' he says. 'At least that's where I think we are. Most people believe there is a limbo between life and death. But for those who study the universe, there's also one between realities and time.'

'How do you know that?'

'I don't, but I just spent the last three days jumping around time and getting stabbed in the gut. I figured everything else must be true, right?'

I fill David in on how right now, in our present, he was involved in the car crash with Audrey and is in a coma. How Liam from the future came to my past and helped me years ago, giving me all the information I would need to try and help them. How Liam and his dad kept his time travelling a secret

168

and knew that David's body was missing in 1993. How the gang is in 2016, worried that David will never wake up, and that I might be missing too. How we have to figure out how to get back home, otherwise we might stay in limbo forever, our bodies never returning to the present.

'Why are you here with me?'

'That's a story that Liam might have to fill you in on, but I always knew I might have to save you. So let's do it. Let's go home.' I smile. 'My job here is so done.'

David raises his eyebrow in disbelief and we both stand at the empty window. 'Just because I might know where we are, doesn't mean I know how to get home.'

'For fuck's sake,' I scream. 'I've really hit my limit of intelligence on this one. I'm done.' I throw my hands up. 'No more theories or talking things out. No more looking and trying to find feelings.' I point to the window. 'It's the only thing here, so let's smash it up and go through it.'

'Smash it with what?' David knocks on the thick glass, proving his point.

On the ground at my feet is a hammer. 'How did that get here?' I ask.

David picks it up and looks at it like it might change into something else. It's small and the blue rubber at the handle is almost blackened with wear and tear.

I glance back at the window, wondering if it would take much smashing to get through, when daylight forms on the other side, clearing the darkness and showing what is waiting on the other side.

Mike and Audrey come into focus first, followed by Stella and Liam, and they appear to be in Mike's living room. I exhale in relief and look at David, who swings his arm back in preparation to hit the hammer right in the centre of the glass pane.

'Stop!' I shout when David is mid swing.

David drops his arm and turns to me. 'What's wrong?' he asks.

'Something's not right,' I say. 'Look at Audrey.' I nod in her direction. 'She's...vibrating. The air around her is moving.' I step closer to the glass, trying to get a sense of what I'm seeing. Audrey is pacing the living room, talking to the others, but the surrounding air seems to pulse, like it's not settled around her.

'What the hell is that?'

'It's not real.' The words are out of my mouth before I've thought them. 'I mean—it doesn't feel real.'

'Then it's not home.' David lowers his arm and hands me the hammer. 'I can't see what you see. Audrey looks fine to me.' He stares at our friends and family on the other side of the glass, talking, and it looks like Audrey is freaking out over something. 'You need to be the one to get us back.'

'What does that mean?'

David nods to the window. 'That's not our reality. But when ours comes by, you'll be able to sense it. Smash the glass and get us home.'

'How do you know all this?' I hiss at the ridiculousness of it all.

'You said you were here to save me. And you seem to have an anchor to what is real.'

'Anchor? How do you know?'

'Everyone has an anchor when it comes to time travel. The problem is—'

'Recognising it. I know. It's what I've been searching for.'

'Well, I guess you found something.'

I look back at the scene and realise that not only is it that there is a visible difference to Audrey, but the entire room on the other side of the glass looks different from what I'm

170

used to. I take a step forward and look past the people at the background of the room. The couch should be closer to the centre of the room. The rug is brown instead of grey. There is a vase of flowers sitting on the side table, but Audrey always insists on keeping flowers in the kitchen so she can see them more often.

When you know what you're looking for, you can see the little decisions that were made differently in this timeline. But the main one for me is Liam. I notice him last, but he's the most powerful difference. He doesn't radiate like he usually does. Liam has a presence about him when you're around him. Like you can feel his warmth even being across from him. That personality that shines out of his smile is duller and subdued. His stance is a little withdrawn and the energy coming from the depth of his bones feels tired and done. This is the Liam I've never met. *This* Liam is the one from the tapes. In essence, it's the same man. The knowledge and intelligence are all still there. The looks and the tattoos and the hair that he wraps tighter in a bun than mine will ever go. But the thing that made Liam from the tapes and my Liam different, I realise, was me. My Liam was part of a couple. My couple. My other half of a lost soul, trying to find its way. This Liam is just as lost as I used to be.

'Me,' I tell David. 'I'm the anchor. I know what to look for now.'

As soon as the words are out of my mouth, it's like someone hit play on a merry-go-round. Scenes of life and daily activities swarm past us as fast as bees on the way back to their queen. Versions of our lives and the people we know are thrown from right to left, only glimpses for us to see the infinite versions of reality that we're alive in. It's impossible to see more than a few seconds as they whiz past, causing my eyes to

171

strain from the repetitiveness of trying to glimpse something tangible I can grapple with.

Instead, I close my eyes and breathe deep through my nose. Inviting the stillness of my meditation routine and the calmness that was here when I first arrived.

When I open my eyes, David is staring at me, and we turn our attention to the window, a slow-motion version of another life that could have been.

Someone who looks exactly like David is the one I notice in the park first. The scene outside the window is a bright sunny day, so bright that we must be somewhere like L.A. or Miami. Nowhere in England ever shines this bright, and the clothes and tall buildings in the background scream American architecture.

The green area is small enough that the twenty or so people here take up most of the room, sitting on the grass. The walkways loop both in front and behind the greenery and lead off to pathways through trees and the start of streets showcasing office buildings and hotels.

'Who are you sitting with?' I ask. David is facing us, and the woman with him has her back to us, as they share lunch and laughter.

David's jaw tightens. 'I don't know. It doesn't matter. It's not home,' he says.

'How do you know? Let's give it a minute and see what happens. Why else would this whole thing slow down and show us? Maybe it's giving us a chance to choose our lives?'

'I don't want this one.' David grits through his teeth. 'Stella is my life. And that's not her.'

He's right. This woman appears to be taller and slimmer, sitting on the grass. Her hair is longer than Stella ever wears it. And I get how you just know someone from a distance.

Even when Liam appeared different to me, I could still recognise him.

I let out a breath before I speak. 'You and Stella were only ever married for like a year.'

David turns to me. 'So?'

'I know you've always loved her.' I hold my hand out to another life that's waiting for him. 'But this might be your chance at happiness, David. Doesn't take a genius to see that you've never been happy since you guys split up.'

'Leave it, Caitlyn.'

I lean forward and lower my voice, scared of what I'm going to say, even though no one else can hear us. 'She took your child from you, David. We all know you've never forgiven her for that.'

David punches the side of the window frame in front of us, screaming. 'Enough.' His hand ricochets off the only tangible thing in this place and he shakes it loose in pain. 'You can't know how much love I still have for her. And the years of stubbornness that kept us apart. But it wasn't her fault. It was mine. And I know that now. It's not a question of forgiving her, it's hoping and praying to god that when we get home, *she* will forgive *me*.'

I nod and turn my attention back to the window. 'So this one's a no go then?' I state as this version of David packs up the trash of his leftover meal.

'How do you think we get this to move along?' I wonder, leaning against the frame. 'Or do you think we have to watch as much as it's going to show us?'

David is leaning on the other side of the frame, staring at the floor. Waiting, like me, for this to be over.

When the alternative version of David grabs a hold of the woman's hand, she spins towards us and they both walk out of the park.

173

'Wait, is that Jessica?' I gasp, staring at my brother's ex-girlfriend, who looks perfectly at ease in this version of reality with his best friend.

David's head snaps up and before he can say anything, the fast-paced, eye hurting, lives swirl past us.

'Ooh.' I make my eyes open as large as they will go and mock horrified shock at David. 'Other you is dating my brother's ex. Shocker.'

David isn't taking the bait like the twenty-year-old I used to know.

'Oh my god.' My shock is real this time. 'Did you and Jessica have a thing?'

'What?' No!' David shakes his head and looks around the dark room for somewhere to sit.

'Chairs would be nice.' I agree, and the magic of limbo provides us with two armchairs, sitting at angles from each other, facing the window of our alternative lives.

'How do you do that?'

I shrug and sit on the seat behind me. 'Would it be too much to ask for popcorn?' I am disappointed when none arrives.

'You want to throw popcorn at the car crash of my life?' David touches his forehead when he speaks.

'Was it terrible?'

'It was Mike and me. We were in the other car that crashed into Audrey.'

I sit forward and reach out for David's hand, but he's too far away and doesn't take mine for the comfort I know he needs. He's spent twenty years on this. On helping Audrey. No one wanted to see her get hurt.

'That's how I started travelling.' David holds up his wrist. 'Liam and I have been working on a harness to help capture lost leap seconds and electric and magnetic pulses that happen in sync with a few other things. *We* never knew if we got it right, but I guess being that close to Audrey, and being involved with the crash that started this all for her, it worked. It really worked.'

'You went all the way to the past to get stabbed?'

David looks me in the eye. 'I went all the way to the past to save Stella's life. Over and over again. Hours and hours of skipping time and landing in a place where she was due to die. Altering and changing things every time so that she would live.'

'Jesus.'

'It's exhausting. And it was right. I love her so much more than I ever thought possible.' David kicks his leg out and the click of his knee reminds me that we're all getting old.

'So when you ask about another woman. If I ever had a thing with Jessica. The answer is no.' He looks at the window of lives whizzing past us. 'In another life, yeah, I could and would see myself with Jessica. I liked her when we met, but she started dating Mike, and that on and off thing they had for years was messy. Besides'—he smiled—'I met Stella right when we moved to L.A., and I have to tell you, when you meet the one, your soulmate that you know your heart and body just belong to. Everything else slips away. Every other crush and likeable person is just a sad grey in comparison.'

I lean forward and get right in his face. 'Then why break her heart and divorce her?' I challenge.

His smile is forced and soft. 'I couldn't face her. Turns out a time-travelling good Samaritan was the one who convinced her to do it.'

'You?' I gasp.

He nods.

'What did you convince her to do?'

175

'The right thing. And then the version of me that had no idea punished her for it.'

'Jesus, why didn't she just explain it all to you when it happened?'

'Because I needed that pain and suffering to pour myself into my work. For it to be the primary focus of my life, so I could figure out all this.' He waves at the window. 'And save her damn life. I need a drink,' he tells me.

'*We* need a drink,' I correct him and place my order with Limbo. Two glasses of ice and a bottle of tequila are delivered along with a small round table that fits neatly between us.

David pours two shots into our glasses and raises his in the air. 'Just so you know, it was all worth it.' He downs his drink and lets out a deep hiss as the alcohol hits the back of his throat.

I pick up the glass in one hand, and rock the hammer in the other. 'You don't think that drinking and choosing a reality to smash our way into is dangerous?'

David smiles. 'It sure is. But what harm is there in looking? Maybe there's a life out there where I never caused Stella so much pain.'

I uncross my legs. 'That better not be the self-pitying reason we're sitting here. I'm not getting stuck in a black hole of limbo while you work through your issues. Suck it up and let's go home.'

David turns to me. 'And what's home for you?' he asks.

CHAPTER
SEVENTEEN

It feels like an hour that we sit in silence, staring at the fast-moving traffic of our lives going past us. Mostly it's so fast we can't make out the specifics, but we get glimpses of people and days, and we can pick out the same people who co-star in our lives.

Most of the lives that look like I'm still alive and happy, I can see Liam either with me, or with the group of people we are with. Sometimes it looks like we're a couple, holding hands or having dinner together, close up and intimate. Other times it looks like we've only met. But he's there. And there is an anticipation that we're about to meet.

I wonder if that's the only life I was ever going to have. Liam is my soulmate and he was always going to be there. Does that mean I have no free will? I swallow thickly and my stomach flips. If I'm destined to be with Liam, then it's the same for him. He's not choosing me any more than I choose him. And I don't want to be with someone who hasn't chosen me. I always knew he was too good for me. That Liam was too smart and too attractive to ever fall for me. But I followed his voice and his advice around like a lovesick puppy for years.

I feel like I've been searching forever. To navigate away from my mother and the things she represents that I hate. And towards a stranger who offered me some hope when I was at my lowest. But once I found them, Liam and the others who *got me*. They understood about never giving up on hope or a lead. Who understood keeping moving and searching. Finally, I wasn't a lone wolf on the hunt, and those few months with Liam were like perfect bliss.

But now I realise you might find your new tribe, but your old one is as much a part of you. It can't be ignored or shut away. It's part of you. Even the parts you wished never existed.

For David things seem to stay the same. It's him and Stella, apart but co-parenting Max, even though David was only married to his mom for a year. Or it's David at a business dinner with Stella and sometimes Mike. Or David working with Liam. Or Jessica. Jessica plays a big part in David's alternative lives. I've counted seven different versions of them as a couple. More that I've seen of him and Stella. He notices it too because he pours himself another drink and pretends not to see it.

It's in the middle of one of their life twists that I bolt forward in my seat and shout, 'Wait.' The mirror stops and plays out the scene that was before us. 'Huh, I had no idea that was going to work,' I say.

'What is it?' David speaks slowly, like he's trying to get the words out clearly.

'Well, first I think we need to switch to coffee. Secondly—' I'm interrupted by the switching out of alcohol for two cups of steamy black goodness.

'Secondly. I know that guy.' I point to Carl Wilson, the author I spent time with in England as part of a research workshop.

Liam and I are both with Carl in what looks like a lab. It's dull and grey and windowless and looks old and dusty. Not at all like David and Liam's workings in the university.

Liam and I are old here. We're both grey-haired and have wrinkles. Not just a little, but our entire faces are covered in them. Liam, of course, still has the manly attractiveness to him. But damn, I look rough.

'Looks like they're building a big one of these.' David holds his wrist up to show off the time anchor that he and David fashioned into a wristwatch. 'That's enough stress to put years on you. Trust me, I know.'

'Huh. I thought he was full of shit.'

David leans closer. 'That looks like a government bunker. See the royal emblazonment in the back?' he asks as he stands.

'Wait,' he says. 'This isn't just a window into alternative lives. It's the future too.'

I stand at the window with David.

'The date on the laptop. It's 2045.'

I nod. The years make sense. Liam and I should both be sixty-five.

David sees me looking at the older version of us. 'Damn, that's you. No offence, but you didn't age with grace.'

David's not wrong. I would imagine if it were him and Stella we were looking at, they would be still dressed to the nines. Hair styled and blemishes at a minimum.

'There's a problem, though. Carl Wilson was the same age when I met him in 2006 in England.'

David moves his attention from me to Carl and back again. 'What do you know about him?' he asks.

'Not a lot, really. He paid me for a consultation on a book he was writing. I was in Ireland for Mike and Audrey's wedding, so it was great timing to jump over to London for a week's work on his novel.'

'Novel on what?'

I shrug. 'All he said was it was a sci-fi and he needed a unique theory to work into a story. I never read the final thing.'

'Wait, back up. How did he even find you?'

I roll my eyes. 'I had like a crazy obsession before I left Blackpool, and I still had access to my old email. He dropped me a mail, and I happened to be online the next day and saw it.'

David narrows his eyes at me. 'Okay, I need all the details on that.'

I groan. 'It was like a few weeks after I got the first tape from Liam and my head was spinning with all the time travel being real, and my potential death, and worst of all, my mum was having an affair.'

'You knew about that back then?'

I shake my head in dismissal of the details. 'I was a bit of a mess. And I wanted to get Liam's attention.' I sit down on the couch and pour myself another coffee. It's still steaming when it comes out of the pot and I relish in the bitter taste to get through the bitter part of my life. 'I realised that being in the past, I could leave behind something that he might see and I could communicate with him. I tried a couple of crazy stunts to get myself in the local newspaper, but honestly, that kind of backfired.'

'What happened?' David's voice is questionably nervous about my answer.

'I climbed Blackpool tower and called the press on myself. People thought I was jumping. I was waiting on the reporter, so I wouldn't come down, and before I knew it, the police had a therapist and negotiator on site to help me.'

David cringes for me and I cover my eyes and groan. 'It was the most embarrassing thing ever,' I confess. 'Because when I realised what was happening, the only thing sixteen-year-old me could think of was to play along.'

'Play along with a suicide attempt?'

'No.' I gasp. 'I just pretended to be talked down, and I had to deal with the therapy afterwards.' I run my hands down my face. 'I had already started dyeing my hair funky colours, and my mum had found my first tattoo.' I stand up and pull my shirt up, showing David the lightning strike on my shoulder and across my back, branching out into blue veins, just like the mark it left on me the night I was struck on the beach. She was convinced that I was having a breakdown. Anyway. The newspaper reported it, but because I was under eighteen, they never printed my name or picture of anything.'

David snickers and I smack him on the knee to shut him up.

'Idea number two wasn't that stupid, but based on my now questionable mental health, it made me look crazy. I started a conspiracy magazine.'

'Stop it, no, you didn't.' He laughs.

'Well, obviously it did the trick.' I wave to the window at our side. 'It might not have got Liam's attention, but it got someone's.'

'What did you put in it?'

I sigh and look up at the blackness where the ceiling should be. 'I should have a copy on my old computer. I can find them for you when we get home. I tried to circulate a few for free in the local shop, but I think most of them ended up in the bin. I had my email on it, because I wanted to know that if Liam ever found one in the future, he could contact me and I would know that it was working. I could answer him in my magazine, and he could write to me in an email. But I got nothing from him. There are physical copies in Blackpool library. It must be where Carl Wilson found them. I had some more information by the time Carl and I met, and mostly, we just talked back and forth. I thought we were just shooting the shit, and he was humouring me as much as I was him.' I wave to the window. 'But obviously he was further involved with real-time travel than I even knew.'

'This is why we're here,' David says. 'It's nothing to do with picking a reality to live in or wondering what could have been. It was all getting us here, to see the future.'

'And what's so important about the future?' I ask.

David stands in front of the glass window and holds up his watch to me. sI can see the mechanics he added that record the leap seconds of time travel. 'He built a fucking time machine.'

The window speeds up, like it thinks we've seen enough, or it's not letting us get off here at this destination and it stops of its own accord at the four of us having dinner in a pub. Liam, Mike, and I, and Mike's ex-girlfriend Jessica is there. Sitting next to David.

'That's what Liam saw when he was a child.' I stand and move towards the glass, hammer in hand, ready to smash my way back to the only recognisable life I want back to. 'We need to get off here and get Mike back to his life with Audrey in L.A.'

David makes no move to stop me when I raise the hammer above my head and I run towards the window, throwing my arm and hammer forward in momentum to smash the window to our lives before us.

The free fall I felt in the elevator earlier is short-lived this time. And it feels more like falling forwards rather than down. Forward and into the seat at the restaurant table is where I fall, David opposite me. By the time I flinch inside my skin, Mike has returned from the bathroom and Liam is mid-conversation with David. I don't know how David managed to continue a conversation after landing in a different version of himself, but he seems flawless while he and Liam continue their friendly argument.

'All I said was, if you had the chance to go back in time and change one thing about your past, would you do it? Would

182

you change it? And more importantly'—David turns to Mike—
'would you let someone change *your* life?'

'What about the ripple effect in people's lives? Who
gets to decide what is *meant to be*?' Liam taps on the table to
underscore his point. 'The experiences and mistakes you have
in life shape who you are. You have no idea what might change
by making sure your spouse made better choices in life,' Liam
argues.

The waitress appears with Mike's birthday cake and
sets it on the table.

'What things in life would you change?' David asks my
brother.

'There's nothing wrong with my life. It's fine the way it
is,' Mike tells him. But it's a lie. In this world, he never met
Audrey, and you can see that the light inside him, the happiness
isn't there.

'You're completely and utterly happy?' David asks.

'I'm not unhappy,' Mike stares at the candles, and in
one breath, blows them out with a whoosh.

The tug behind me alerts me to the switch that Liam
has spoken so often about. I turn my head, looking for the ten-
year-old boy who witnessed this in a time jump to the future
once, and I find him. Sitting at the table next to us, alone and
lost, he's fading out in a ball of lightning, just as I'm being pulled
backwards. Flying, like an unstrapped passenger, about to be
launched full speed out of a vehicle.

Find my anchor. That was what I was always trying to
do. To the world, to the earth or reality or whatever this was.
But it wasn't one thing, it was everything.

183

I am everything in my own life. I'm the centre of my own universe, and I can save myself. But I can also save the others who have no idea what's happening. I reach my arms out, flying forward with nothing to capture but air. I will everyone to come along with me. For Liam, David, and Mike all to come with me back to the reality we lived in. Back to where we can save Audrey from the crash we've left her in. Back to Stella and Ethan. Back to a world where we can all work together and find out how to control this thing once and for all. To see what the hell Carl Wilson was really writing about, and his plans for the future.

To see my future. A place where I no longer have to fear an early death. Where I can be something and someone important. Where I can see if Liam really wants to fall in love with me, with no interference from destiny.

I wake in my brother's house in L.A., standing in the kitchen near the sink.

The tap is running, and I must have been doing something for the kids. If I'm back where I should be, when I should be, it's my brother's fortieth birthday, and he is off saving his wife from a car crash. Liam and David should be there, too. Liam was always going to be close by to help with anything medical while an ambulance was called, and hopefully David is back where he needs to be too.

My phone rings, and I spin fast, trying to locate the sound that I thought was lost a thousand feet below me in a cave. On the kitchen table at the other end of the room, my phone vibrates off the tabletop in an angry cry before cutting off. The time on my screen shows 11.11 a.m. I've been gone for about ten minutes.

A text message appears on my screen and I read the first part of it from Liam.

We're all okay. I need to know you are, too.

184

One thing I found from this whole thing. There is a version of the future out there, where Liam and I get to grow old and grey together. And despite what might happen with Carl Wilson and us in the future, I'm banking on the fact I'm going to live the rest of my life with Liam.

I think I might rest now. I text back.

Hell no, woman. We're only getting started. We have work to do.

A note from the
AUTHOR

Did you know the best way you can support an author is to leave a review? If you enjoyed this novel, please take a few minutes to leave your rating on your platform of choice. I appreciate the support!

Enjoy this story? Want FREE deleted scenes from the novel? Want Giveaways? Advanced Reader Copies? Exclusive sneak peeks of future chapters?

Sign up to my mailing list (I promise not to spam you) and keep up to date on future releases and claim your first FREEBIE! bronamills.com

Subscribe to my newsletter for exclusive free giveaways, news on what's coming next, book covers and character development and sneak peeks at chapters before they are released!

Follow me on social media
instagram.com/bronamillsauthor
tictok.com/@bronamills
facebook.com/bronamillsauthor

Or join up to my readers group
www.facebook.com/groups/120622995251578

CONTINUE THE SERIES

The Accidental Time Traveller - Book One
Time Traveller - Book Two
War and books - A Companion Romance Novel - Book 2.5
On A Time Travel Mission – Book Three
Once Upon a Timeloop - Book Four

Other Books by the author

The Saving Dystopia series: Time Glitch - A Saving Dystopia Story